CW00470280

Tempting Tricks

A Tempting Nights Romance
Book Two

MICHELLE WINDSOR

First published February 2019

Published by
Windsor House Publishing
Cover design by Amanda Walker Design Services
Editing provided by Kendra Gaither at Kendra's Editing and Book Services

WARNING
This book contains elements of PTSD and suicide.

For all our soldiers.

Thank you for your service and your sacrifices.

CHAPTER ONE

~Trick~

I walk down the dimly lit hallway, ignoring everyone I pass along the way, my destination already decided before I even arrive. I tried to stay away tonight. I really did. I drank a quarter bottle of Patron in the hope I'd slip into some kind of unconscious slumber in an attempt to stay away. It didn't work. I still couldn't shut out the images that play like a movie in my head when I close my eyes.

So, here I am, in the one place I know I can lose myself. The one place I know can give me something else to focus on. Something else besides the demons always lurking in the recesses of my mind, always reminding me that I shouldn't be here. I should be with them, burnt ash forever lost in the desert sands of Iraq.

I stop when I reach the entrance to my salvation, nodding at the door keeper. No one goes into this room unless they've been approved beforehand. His name is Gus, and he knows me well enough to know, if I'm standing in front of this door, I'm in need of something more. More than I usually come looking for. He looks me up and down, his eyes cold and detached, and then speaks. "Weren't you just here a couple days ago?"

"Yep." That's it. That's all he's getting unless he asks for more. It's my goddamn body to do whatever I want with.

"You even healed yet?" His eyes squint as he tries to assess my physical condition to determine if I can handle what happens if he lets me through to the other side.

"I want more. I'm ready." I *need* more. I *crave* more. I *deserve* more.

He doesn't budge. It's a clear indication that my answer isn't enough. I puff out a long, slow breath through my nostrils, then pull my shirt over my head. I keep it clutched in my hand as I lift my arms out to my sides and slowly turn in a circle, stopping when I'm facing him again.

"You've still got scabs." His eyes roam over my chest.

"I'm fine," I reply, my voice flat and devoid of emotion.

He tilts his head once toward the door, my approval to enter. "Only because Mistress Blue doesn't mind a little bit of blood."

I keep my shirt off, my fingers crushing the soft material into a tight ball as I walk by to push through the door. "Good, 'cause neither do I."

As soon as I'm on the other side, I take three steps to a padded black mat and fall to my knees, bowing my head as I rest my hands on the tops of my thighs. I've just given my submission to whomever wants it in this room. Any free will

I have, any desires I have, any fears I have no longer exist or matter. In here, they belong to someone else to control, to harness, to use in any way they want. For their pleasure, not mine. My only pleasure will be in the pain. I just pray it's enough to make me forget for a little while.

Goosebumps break out across my flesh when shiny, latex boots step into my vision. My eyes lift and lock onto black fingernails clutched around the handle of a cat-o-nine tails. But this isn't your typical whip. It's made of rope instead of leather, with each end knotted tightly. People think leather hurts, but the bite rope takes out of your skin is so much more punishing. My cock twitches to life when she lifts the whip and drags it across my bare back.

"Has Halloween come early?" Her sultry voice drips down to my ears. "I didn't even have to say Trick or Treat." She lowers herself, turning the handle of the whip, placing it under my chin, and lifting it until my eyes are even with hers. "My lucky day or yours?"

"Hopefully mine." Her brow quirks up at my reply as she stands, releasing the hold the handle has on my chin.

"Get up." The sultry tone is gone, replaced with a venom I'm hoping will deliver what I need.

I rise to my feet immediately, my eyes still lowered. My nostrils flare as I absorb the scents permeating the room. Salty sweat, the clean smell of burning wax, and the tangy aroma of blood, the strongest of them all, causing my dick to fully harden. She barks for me to undress completely, and I do, quickly, leaving my clothing in a heap on the floor.

"I love that you come with your very own attachment." She purrs, grasping the heavy metal ring I have pierced through my left nipple, tugging it sharply before fastening a thick silver chain to it. She turns, pulling the makeshift leash, forcing me to follow behind her, yanking hard if I fall too far behind. Which, sometimes I do, just because I like the way it feels.

Her boots clunk to a loud stop as she plants one foot and spins around. She gathers the chain, wrapping it slowly around her wrist, forcing me forward until I'm inches from her body. Lavender invades my nostrils when I inhale, the scent overwhelming when she lowers her head and sinks her teeth into my earlobe. She tugs once, hard, before releasing the tender flesh, her tongue dragging over her bite mark. "Just having you in my snare makes me so wet."

I reach my hand between her legs and skim two fingers up the inside of her thigh. I'm about to confirm her disclosure, but before I can, I feel the knots of the whip smack across my back. I drop to my knees, a moan falling from my rounded lips, my eyes rolling back in pleasure. This. This is what I want.

"Did I give you permission to touch me?" She lifts her foot and places the pointy heel of the boot against my thigh.

I shake my head. I know what the answer is supposed to be, but if I want all that she has to offer, I can't give her that. I want her to punish me, after all. "I thought you wanted me to touch you, Mistress."

She leans forward, pushing her body into the heel, the weight making the skin around the tip pucker and finally break, small trails of blood seeping out, trickling down my leg. "I tell you what I want. When to touch me. How to touch me."

There's the bite of the whip against the bare flesh on my back again. I sigh out my consent, my head bowed, "Yes, Mistress." My cock throbs its contentment against my bowed stomach.

"Get up!" The sting of rope slices across my chest as I rise. "Against the wall." I turn, rewarded with another slash of the whip against my buttocks as I walk to the cross hanging in front of me. The next twenty minutes are a blur of pleasure and pain. The whip falls against my skin again and again. Her mouth teases my cock before she finally frees me, my body crumpling at her feet. Her grip on my cock rough as she drags me to the bed then climbs on top of me. Her wet core thrusts onto my hardness. She grinds her hips against me, sliding her body against mine, my blood a thin, wet layer between us, before we both scream out our releases. And I finally freefall into utter bliss, blacking out, forgetting everything for just a little while.

~Annabelle~

He's quiet. He's always quiet. He's been sitting there for thirty minutes with barely six words spoken. Single word answers to questions I've asked. I know he hates coming to these sessions, and only does because it's a requirement to get his pilot license reinstated. I've come to loathe this time as well, but not for the same reason as him. I lift my right leg off my left, uncrossing them, the bare skin sticking together briefly as I pull them apart. I shift so that

I'm sitting up straighter and then cross my legs again, this time left over right. There's a small red circle on the top of my left leg, just above my knee. It's the spot my other leg was resting on before I repositioned. I stare at it a moment and then swing my attention back to my client, noticing his eyes are trailing up the length of my bare legs.

Instead of saying anything, I drag my eyes slowly down his frame. He's more relaxed than me, his jean clad legs stretched in front of him, ankles crossed above worn leather work boots. One hand rests loosely on his thigh while the other is clenched in a fist on the arm of the chair, betraying his actual comfort level. My eyes skim up his arm, noticing the tattoo sneaking out from under the short sleeve of the shirt, before moving across his chest, where I lock onto the piercing I can make out under the thin material. I squeeze my legs together as I feel my core contract. I have to restrain myself from licking my lips as I wonder, for only an instant, what it would feel like to have that ring between my teeth. He clears his throat, bringing me back to my senses, my gaze swinging to his, but not before I notice something near the collar of his shirt.

"You're bleeding." I lift my hand as I rise from my chair, pointing to the stain of blood seeping through his shirt.

He looks down, frowns, and then lifts his eyes back to mine, shrugging. "I'm fine."

"You're not fine if blood is soaking through your shirt," I state matter-of-factly and stride past him into the private bathroom. I open the cabinet under the sink to pull out the first aid kit, carrying it back over to where he's still sitting casually. I set it on the table next to him and open it up.

"It's nothing, Doc." His lips purse tightly as I open a piece of gauze, moving toward the stain on his shirt, then freeze, my hand hovering. I realize I either need to lift his shirt up, or slide the gauze under the neck of the material to cover the wound. If it was any other client, I probably wouldn't have hesitated. But this one, this one makes me feel things I know I shouldn't. His eyes slide up and lock onto mine as he pinches the gauze from my fingers. He slides it under the collar of the shirt to press against his skin.

I realize my hand is still lingering over him and take a quick step back, standing straight as I do. One side of his mouth cocks up as a chuckle vibrates lightly from his chest. He knows he's making me nervous, and it pisses me off, so I do the one thing I shouldn't as his doctor and go on the offensive.

"You went back again, didn't you?"

He pulls the bloodied gauze out from under his shirt, balling it up into a wad, then rises. He strolls over to the trash can located next to my desk to drop it in before finally responding. "So?"

"So, I thought we agreed you were going to find another way to try to deal with the memories." I walk over to my desk, leaning back against it.

He ambles around the desk until he's in front of me. He faces me and shrugs, crossing his arms. "This is what works best for me."

I push off the desk and stand up straight because I don't like him looking down at me as we talk. It makes me feel less in control. "Letting someone beat you to the point where you're still bleeding the next day is what works?"

He glares at me, his arms flexing before he grins widely, surprising me. "I like it. It feels good."

"You take pleasure in being punished?"

He scoffs. "No."

My brows arch in confrontation. "No?"

There is a long pause before he responds, his voice even, devoid of emotion. "I take pleasure in the pain."

"In the pain? How? How does pain equate to pleasure?" I unconsciously lean forward, wanting to be closer to him, to truly understand how this could possibly be the case.

"Because it's better."

"Better than what?" I'm still confused and surprise myself with the sharp bite of my retort. I force myself to lean back, blowing a long breath of air through lips that are barely open.

His eyes lock back onto mine, the green of his irises so dark and intense they remind me of pine branches whipping wildly in the fierce winter winds. "Better than everything else."

This doesn't surprise me. Other patients have told me that inflicting physical pain onto themselves takes away the mental pain they are feeling, even if it's just for a short amount of time. To them, that time is pure bliss.

I smile sadly and nod my head in understanding but still try to reason with him. "Patrick, we have to find another way. A better way. A way that doesn't leave you bloody and battered."

He stares at me, and I can see a million thoughts are running through his mind, but he doesn't tell me any of them. Instead, I watch as he unfolds his arms and takes three steps forward, closing the gap between us, leaving him inches from me. He's invading my space, and instead of moving back, I look up and meet his gaze, the hair on the back of my neck standing on end from the electricity sparking between us. I can hear my own breath coming out in short pants. I know, without it being said, that he has another way to feel better and all I have to do is say yes. I'm not sure how long we stand there, the tension between us growing, when the bell from the timer dings. I jump, his hand snaking out, wrapping around my wrist. "Easy." He leans an inch closer, his breath hot on my ear as he whispers, "Time's up." Then he turns abruptly and strides out of my office, slamming the door behind him.

CHAPTER TWO

~Trick~

I'm a quarter of the way down the hallway before the door slams shut behind me, my heart banging against my chest as I stride past the elevator and burst through the doorway to the staircase. I'm on the twenty-third floor, but right now, I don't give a damn. I fly down the steps, not stopping until I've reached the twelfth-floor landing, finally feeling like I've put enough distance between myself and Doctor Murphy.

Placing my balled hands onto the wall, I rest my head on my bicep. I blow out a breath of air to try to slow down my racing heart. At least, running down twelve flights of stairs has lessened the ache throbbing between my legs. Being in the same room with her is getting harder and harder. Especially when she wears a skirt like she did today, exposing her long, bare legs. Perfectly smooth, like pale silk, except for the tiny rose tattoo she has on one ankle, a petal falling softly beside a thorny stem.

"Get your shit together, man!" I yell, my words echoing against the cement tunnel of the staircase. I push myself off the wall, rake one hand through my already tousled brown mop, and begin descending the stairs again. This time, at a slower pace. Therapy is supposed to be helping me, but each time I leave, I only feel more frustrated. What I'd really like to do is lay her back on her desk, push her skirt up, spread those long legs, and sink deep inside her. That's a therapy session I could get on board with. And I know for a fact I'd feel a fuck of a lot better than I do right now.

I reach the first floor and push through the door, emerging into a corner of the lobby, and my phone rings. I pull it out of my pocket, see it's Trey and hit accept to take the call. "What's up?"

"It's me, not Trey," Charlotte, Trey's fiancée and soon-to-be baby momma, says. I like her. She makes my best friend happy, and working in the medical profession like him makes them a good fit. She's six months pregnant with their little girl and lives one floor below mine in the same apartment building.

"Hey, Charlie." I pull the phone away from my ear to check that I didn't misread the call when it came in. "Why are you calling from Trey's phone? Is everything okay? Is the baby okay?"

"Yes, yes, everything's fine." She laughs lightly. "If only you would show others how much of a big caring teddy bear you really are. Trey's phone was just closer than mine, and I was too lazy to push this big ole belly off the couch."

"Okay, what's up? Another craving?" I drawl out as I exit the building, a blast of frigid March air reminding me that I left my jacket up in her damn office. "Fuck!"

"Trick!" Charlie's worried voice carries over the phone. "Are you okay?"

I stomp my foot on the ground in frustration, making an instant decision. I'd rather freeze my balls off then go back into the same room with Doctor Murphy right now. I turn in the direction I just came from and walk back into the lobby. "Yep, sorry. Just realized I forgot something."

"Are you sure?" She asks, not convinced. "Where are you?"

"Charlie, what do you need? Did you call for something?" I'm short with her. I know I am. But I've already got one woman driving me fucking nuts today, I don't need another.

"I just wanted to know when you were going to be home," she says quietly. "I have something for you. I went up to your place, but you weren't there."

Great, now I feel like shit for snapping at her. "Sorry, Charlie. Bad morning. I'm on my way home now. You need anything?"

"No, just text me when you're home. I'll come up." There's a pause before she continues. "You sure you're okay?"

"Yeah, yeah." I've softened my tone considerably, feeling like a total douche bag for snapping at her in the first place. "I'm good. I'm gonna catch a cab. Should be there shortly."

"Okay, see ya soon." She ends the call, and I slide my phone back into my pocket, pulling my cash out to see what

I've got on me. Thirty bucks. Plenty for a taxi. No fucking way I'm going up to get my jacket, and no way I'm walking home without one.

Twenty minutes later, I step out onto the seventh floor of my building and turn left to Trey and Charlie's apartment instead of going up to mine. I knock when I reach the door, my head cocking when I hear a commotion on the other side, Charlie yelling at Trey to get the door. *What the hell is she up to now?*

The door swings wide, Trey on the other side, a crooked smile on his scruffy face. "I just want you to know I had nothing to do with this." He motions for me to come in.

"What the fuck?" I enter their living room and shoot him a questioning look. "She planning an intervention or something?"

"Yeah, a pussy intervention." He chuffs out a laugh, running a hand over his stubbled chin in thought. "Actually, this will probably help get you more of that."

One side of my mouth shoots up in a devilish grin. "Okay, now I'm intrigued."

"Is he ready?" Charlie's voice shouts out from behind the bedroom door.

"Sweetie, he's here. What else do you want him to do?" Trey walks a couple steps closer to the door she's behind. "Close his eyes?" The last part is dripping with sarcasm, but it's no surprise when she responds.

"Yes! And have him sit on the couch!" She's little, but boy, she's bossy.

I shoot Trey a look, throwing my hands up to my side. "What the fuck is going on?"

He shakes his head and replies in a pleading voice, "Just do what she says, man. Help me out here."

"You're so fucking pussy whipped, dude." I roll my eyes but throw the guy a bone and go sit on the couch.

"Close your eyes," Trey hisses out.

"Jesus Christ," I mutter, but close them, crossing my arms over my chest.

"Okay, Charlie, he's ready," Trey calls out.

I hear the door click open and then the patter of footsteps growing louder as she approaches and then stops in front of me. I feel the warm weight of something round being placed in my lap and instinctively lower my hands just as Charlie yells, "Surprise!"

My eyes snap open to look down as my fingers land on soft fur. I nearly jump up when I realize what I'm holding but am too afraid I'm going to drop it on the floor.

"It's a boy!" Charlie jumps in place and claps her hands. "Congrats, Daddy!"

"What the ever-loving fuck?" My eyes dart to her then the fur ball on my lap, my nostrils flaring as I try not to yell when I glare back up at her. "This is a puppy, Charlie."

"More to the point, it's your puppy." She beams angelically at me. "A Siberian Husky. Known to be intelligent, independent, and stubborn." Her brows arch as she continues, her tone changing to one of contention. "I thought you'd make the perfect match."

"What the hell am I going to do with a puppy?" I stand, grabbing the bundle of fur in my hands, and hold it in front of her. "Take it back."

She takes a step away, clasping her hands behind her. "Nope." She looks down at the puppy, now awake and squirming to try to get out of my grasp. "Trick, you can't hold him like that!"

I grasp it a little tighter to stop it from wriggling out of my hands and thrust it toward her again. "Then take it!"

She shakes her head firmly and stomps a foot. "No! This will be good for you. You need something to love."

Tired of trying to stop the damn puppy from falling, I gather it against my torso and hold it there, shooting Charlie a hurt look. "I love lots of things."

Her brow lifts as she crosses her arms. "Name one thing. Besides Trey and me."

"When did I ever say I loved you?" One side of my mouth cocks up into a grin as I challenge her.

She doesn't take the bait. Instead, she moves beside me and sits on the couch, patting the space next to her. "Some homeless guy had this whole litter of puppies over on Eleventh, near DeWitt Park. If they don't freeze to death, sooner or later, they'll probably starve. I couldn't just walk by and not try to do something to help."

"Then you keep it." I sit, shoving the puppy onto her lap. "I can't take care of a damn dog."

"No." She shifts the squirming ball of fur back over to my lap. "I got him for you. Trey and I will have a new baby here in a few months. We can't get a dog right now."

"Oh, but I can?" The little beast sinks his teeth playfully

into my finger when I try to move it back to her lap again. "Ouch!" I pull my wounded digit from its mouth. "He's got sharp little fangs!"

"Those are love bites." She reaches over and pats the puppy on the head. "Good boy." Then she smiles back up at me. "What are you going to name him?"

I groan. "Come on, Charlie." I look down as the puppy begins licking the finger he was biting just moments ago. I feel myself begin to thaw when piercing blue eyes look up at me. "I don't have time for a pet."

"Don't be silly." She stands again and walks over to the kitchen counter. "The only time you ever leave that apartment is to go to The Den or for one of your Temptation dates. Let's face it, you really can do without either of those things in your life."

"I disagree. Fucking is the highlight of my life," I retort smugly. I feel a hard smack to the back of my head.

"Hey, asshole, watch how you speak to my girl." Trey moves in front of me and points to the puppy. "Try him out for a week. Maybe he'll keep you."

I look down at the little guy again, his large puppy paws playing with the leather cord I have wrapped around my wrist. "I don't even know what the hell to feed him."

"No problem!" Charlie is back in front of me, setting a big bag on the coffee table, and begins pulling items out of it. "I sent Trey to the pet store and we got you covered." I watch as she shows me what they got. "A collar, a leash, some dog bowls, a puppy bed, and oh!" She looks up at Trey adoringly. "I didn't tell you to get this!" She lifts a small stuffed candy cane out of the bag and gives it to the puppy, who grips it in his jaw immediately.

Trey just shrugs and mumbles. "It was on sale. Trying to get rid of all the Christmas stock."

She blows him a kiss then turns her attention back to rustling through the bag but doesn't lift anything else out. "And there's food, puppy pads, and poopy bags for you, too."

"Puppy pads?" I ask, not sure I want to know the answer.

She places her hands on her hips. "Really, Trick?" She shakes her head. "You'll need to enclose him in a small area when you aren't home, like the bathroom, and put these down on the floor in case he needs to go to the bathroom."

"Yeah, just what I want to be doing in my spare time, Charlie." I stand and peer into the bag. "Is there a book in there on how to take care of this thing? 'Cause I ain't got a fucking clue."

Charlie claps her hands, her mouth breaking into a wide smile. "So, you'll take him?"

I grumble. "You really aren't giving me much of a choice here, are you?" I lift the squirming monster up and turn him so we're face to face. "I guess we're stuck with each other." He lunges forward and laps his tongue over my cheek, I think in approval, and I can't help but laugh.

"See? He loves you already!" Charlie exclaims, joy in her voice.

"Sorry, man." Trey claps a hand against my shoulder. "I tried to talk her out of it, but you know how she is once she makes up her mind." He starts loading everything back into the bag and grabs it by the handles. "Come on, I'll go up with you."

I stuff the little beast under my arm, pick up the stuffed toy, and fix my eyes on Charlie. “I’ll give him one week.” Then I stride past her to the door, Trey on my heels.

“You’re welcome!” she sing-songs as we exit, clearly knowing I’ve already lost this battle.

CHAPTER THREE

~Annabelle~

I unlock the door to my apartment, dump my bags unceremoniously on the floor as I enter, then turn to relock the door behind me. It's not that I live in a bad neighborhood, but I do live alone and have always erred on the side of caution. Something ingrained in me by my father once upon a time.

"Nyla." I toe off my sneakers, leaving them by the door as well, and walk further into the apartment as I call out again, "Hey, Nyla, Momma's home." I smile, bending down as my gray tiger kitty appears out of nowhere and weaves between my feet, purring loudly. I stroke her soft fur and bend to plant a few kisses on her head. She rears up on her back legs and butts her head against my mouth in return. "Did you miss me, baby? You sure are a love bug tonight."

I stand, glancing at her food dish, and notice it's empty.

Ah, the real reason for all the love; she wants me to feed her. "Come on then."

I walk to the cupboard to pull down a can of food. After opening it, I pull a fork out of the drawer before moving back to the bowl to scoop out the contents of the can. She gives me one final rub against the leg in thanks and then dives into her food. "Enjoy, baby."

I drop the can in the trash, set the fork in the sink, then walk back over to the door to remove and hang my coat up in the small closet off my kitchen. I need a shower. I went to the gym after my last patient and put in a grueling workout. I'm still sweaty, and I'm sure I stink. But my curiosity gets the better of me, so I stoop next to the bags on the floor and pull out the worn leather bomber jacket I shoved in my large purse before leaving the office.

What the hell am I doing? This is wrong on so many levels. I should have just left it hanging on the coat rack in my office. For when he comes next time. But here I am, in my own apartment, holding his jacket in my hands. I raise it slowly to my nose and inhale, pressing it against my face, my lids closing. It smells like him. Or, at least, like he smelled today when he was looming over me, almost pressing his body against mine. Warm and musky and slightly spicy. A flush of heat runs through my veins when I remember the way his hot breath felt against my ear.

I open my eyes slowly and lower the jacket. I have seriously lost my marbles. I'm the one who needs therapy now. But I can't seem to stop myself and the incessant need I have to know more about him, since he certainly isn't opening himself up to me. I carry the coat with me over to the couch and sit. I lay the coat flat on my lap and am about to unzip one of the front pockets when there's a loud knock on my door, startling me into an upright position, the coat slipping off my lap to the floor.

There are usually only two people who come knocking on my door unannounced. I stride over to the door and peer into the peep hole, my brows furrowing. I step back, unlock and pull the door wide. "Holly, what's the matter?"

She enters, strolls by, drops a quick kiss on my cheek, and continues to the kitchen. "Why would anything be the matter? Can't I just drop in?"

I follow, watching as she sets a bottle of wine and a bag of some kind of take-out, I'm guessing Thai by the smell, on the counter. "Because when you show up with wine and food, it generally means you're fighting with Billy again."

She shrugs, making her way around the counter to grab the corkscrew out of a drawer. "Billy's an asshole."

"I've been telling you that for six months."

"I need to break up with him." She reaches for the bottle on the counter and begins the process of screwing the opener into the cork.

"I've also been telling you that for six months," I repeat dryly.

"He's just so god damn good in bed." The cork pulls out with a loud pop, causing us both to laugh out loud.

"Well, sex isn't everything." I approach the counter and begin opening the square brown bag to see what she's brought.

"Ha!" Holly snorts. "Says the girl who hasn't had sex in what? A year?"

"Shut up!" I pull containers out of the bag, Thai as suspected, and slam them down on the marble. "Just because I haven't had sex in *ten months*—" I glare at her pointedly, "not a year, thank you very much, doesn't mean I don't know what good sex is."

"Listen, Belle, if you were getting good sex, really good sex, even if the guy was an asshole, you'd probably put up with half the shit I do, too." She fills two wine glasses, grabs a couple forks, and carries them all into the living room.

I sigh, following with the food. "Maybe you're right." I sit next to her on the couch and place the food on my coffee table. "But, unfortunately, I only seem to get the asshole part of the equation. None of the guys I've dated do anything for me in bed."

"See?" She points her fork at me, a long noodle dangling from the tines. "You don't know good sex yet."

My eyeballs roll heavily to the ceiling, but I don't disagree with her again. She's probably right. I've certainly never had a guy give me an orgasm without some other kind of stimulation involved. Sex just always seemed like a necessary inconvenience with the men I was with, so it just seemed easier to stop dating. "So, you wanna talk about what happened between you and Billy?"

"Nope." She takes a big gulp of her wine. "Same old shit. I'm pretty sure he's screwing some girl in his office." She looks up at me and sighs. "I really do need to break up with him."

I laugh and nod my head. There's no point in telling her again that I agree. One thing I've learned about Holly in the six years we've been friends, she'll leave when she's good and ready. And when she does, it's done. No crying. No muss. No big scene. She just moves on. I so wish I could be like that. I wallow for weeks and wonder about every little thing I may have done wrong.

"Do you have something you want to tell me?" She looks over at me and then down at the jacket on the floor. "'Cause that sure don't look like something you'd wear."

I feel my cheeks heat as I wave my hand and try to dismiss her question casually. "Oh, that's a patient's. He forgot it in my office."

"And you brought it home because?"

So much for trying to brush it off. "Oh, I was thinking I might drop it off tomorrow. He doesn't live too far from here, and he doesn't have another appointment with me until Friday."

"Nope." She leans over and pulls the jacket off the floor. "I can tell just by the look on your face that you're hiding something."

I put my food on the table and grab the sleeve of the jacket, trying to yank it back from her. "Don't be ridiculous!" I tug again. "Give me that!"

"Uh-uh!" She tugs even harder, ripping it completely from my grasp. "You're hiding something!" Her eyes are sparkling at the knowledge that she's caught me at something. "Tell me!"

I groan and throw a hand over my face. "This is so unethical, Holly!"

"Oh. My. God." She yelps. "You had sex with a patient!" Instead of disgust though, her face is filled with delight.

I slap her on the arm. "No!" Then I lower my head into

my hands, mumbling, "But I've sure thought about it a few times."

"Annabelle Murphy!" She giggles. "How unbelievably unprofessional of you!" Holly is a hairdresser, so she's never going to be in the same boat as me. "Tell me *everything!*"

I reach for my wine and take a fortifying gulp. "There's nothing to tell. I mean, he's gorgeous in that tall, dark, and deadly kind of way. He just transferred to me about five weeks ago, with some serious PTSD issues we're trying to deal with, but he's not opening up. So, I mainly just sit there for most of our sessions, staring at him, staring at me." I look up at her, my cheeks flushing again. "I mean, he's really good-looking, Holly. Dark brown hair, piercing green eyes, and he has this nipple ring that has me—"

"Whoa!" She sits up straight, her hand slapping down on my knee. "How the hell do you know he has a nipple ring? I thought you hadn't slept with him?"

"Because I can see it through some of the t-shirts he wears. I swear to God, he does it on purpose. Like he knows he's driving me mad."

"Girl, you need to assign him to a new therapist and then find that man and get busy with him."

"Believe me, it's crossed my mind." I scowl and blow out a breath. "I certainly don't feel like I'm making much progress with him."

"So, why do you have his jacket?" She lifts it up off her lap then drops it back down again.

"I don't know. I was curious. I wanted to see if it gave me any clues to who he is, what he does, where he goes." I look up at her and throw my hands up. "Is that the most pathetic thing you ever heard?"

Her eyes lock with mine as she crinkles her nose. "Honey, I've heard and seen a lot worse." Then she bends down, inhales, and looks back up at me. "And Jesus, if he smells as good as this coat, I get it." She starts shuffling the coat around, stopping when she finds one of the pockets, her eyes darting back up to mine. "Should we?"

"This is so wrong," I whisper, but nod my head up and down at the same time.

"Well, technically, I'm doing the snooping, if that makes you feel any better." She winks, unzips the pocket, and slides her hand inside, pulling it out a second later, several items between her fingers. She releases her hold, dropping everything on the couch between us. I look and take it in. A pack of gum, a condom, and some kind of card. We look at each other, equally unimpressed. "Well, he has the important things covered; fresh breath and protection."

We both laugh, some of our nerves dissipating with the realization that we haven't made any real breach to his privacy. Holly reaches out and turns the card over, then rears back. "Oh! Well, this is interesting."

"What?" I grab the card out of her hand. It's a membership card, with his name, picture, and an identification number to some place called The Den. I look up at her. "What's The Den?"

"It's an underground BDMS club." She snags the card out of my fingers and holds it up again. "He *is* hot!"

I grab it back from her and hold it against my chest like it needs protecting. "How in the world do you know about a sex den?"

She laughs and rolls her eyes at me. "It's not a sex den. It's just a club where you can go to meet other people who might like to do things that you like to do."

"What kind of things?" I feel like an idiot asking her these questions. I've seen Fifty Shades of whatever, so I'm not totally oblivious that there's more than missionary sex happening out there, but I didn't know there were clubs right here in the city where you could go and actually do that sort of thing.

Holly takes a slug of her wine and continues. "Oh, you know, bondage, or ménage, or maybe another woman, or maybe you're into someone whipping you."

My eyes fly wide when realization dawns that this is where Patrick must go to receive the punishment he tells me he enjoys. "Do you go there? How do you know so much about this?" I sit up and lean closer to my friend, wanting to know everything.

"Let's just say that vanilla sex doesn't really do it for me, and leave it at that." She looks down into her wine glass before lifting it to her crooked lips to drain the rest of the glass. "Want more?" She rises and heads to the kitchen.

"Um, hell yes. I need more!"

Somehow, after our second glass of wine, we end up on The Den's website. Holly gives me a tour of the different rooms that can be visited there, and instead of feeling disgusted, I'm surprised when I feel myself getting turned on. I shift in my seat at the counter and grip my wine glass as I take another gulp in relief.

"Oh!" Holly points to a calendar of events that's pulled up on the screen. "They're having a demo night. This Thursday!" She turns to me and shoves her shoulder up against mine. "We should go! How much fun would that be?"

My heart starts racing at the idea of it, but I brush off her suggestion with a nervous laugh. "I could never! What if Patrick happened to be there? That would be awful!"

"Would it really?" she asks, smirking. "You could wear a costume. Everyone is pretending to be someone else while they're there anyway."

"Yes, I'll just throw on my leather dress and boots, wear a wig, and saunter in there. No one will ever know it's me."

"I'll totally do your hair! I have a blonde wig that would be perfect on you!" She claps her hands in delight at the thought of dolling me up.

"I was joking, Holly," I deadpan, my heart fluttering wildly in my chest at the very thought of being in that kind of room, doing those kinds of things, with possibly the one man I shouldn't be.

CHAPTER FOUR

~Trick~

"Come on, Trick. You'll come to Dubai with me after this, right?" My co-pilot, Wiley Coyote, pleads with me.

I give him a side-grin and shake my head. "No go, Coyote. I've got two more weeks and I'm headed state-side. I've had enough middle-eastern pussy to last me a lifetime."

"Ah shit, Trick, you ain't seen nothing 'til you see what they got in—"

"RPG! Seven o'clock! Bank hard right, Captain!" Tripp, my left gunner shouts. "Right! Right! Right!"

I maneuver a hard right and dive at the same time in hopes of evading the flying missile, look over my shoulder and realize it's too late. "Brace for impact!" I shout to my crew. "Call it in, Coyote!"

"Fuck!" My neck and head jerk forward, my helmet

slamming into the windshield as I feel us begin to spin. "We're hit!" I clutch the stick in my hand, turning it to try to regain control, but we just keep spinning and spinning. "Fuck! Hold on, guys!" I yell a second before we slam into the ground and begin rolling.

"Ahhhhh!" I scream, snapping awake in pain.

"Hold on, buddy." I look up to see Coyote's face over me, his hands hooked under my arms as he drags me across the hot desert sand, and I remember the crash.

"Let me up, Coyote!" I struggle to stand and feel a lightning bolt of pain shoot up my leg. "Fuck!"

"I think your leg's broke, Cap." He continues dragging me, and I can see the chopper in front of me, flames shooting up from the tail end.

I shrug him off to try to stand and end up on my ass again. I need to get my men out of that helicopter! "Fuck! I can't fucking stand, Wiley!" I look at him, fear and anger fringing the edges of my voice. "Leave me! Go get them!"

He nods and sprints back to the chopper as I try to stand again and fail. I start dragging myself across the sand toward the chopper. I have to do something. My heart thumps against my chest, blood coursing through my veins, sweat pouring down my forehead, the salt stinging my eyes. I look up, and through the blur, I can see Coyote climbing up into the chopper. Then all I see is fire; red flames spread everywhere, right before a huge explosion rocks the earth underneath me and destroys what's left of my crew.

"*No!!!*" I sit up, my own scream jerking me awake. I pant out quick breaths, blinking rapidly to adjust to the light in the room. I'm home. I'm safe. I'm alive. I hang my head at this last thought and drop my head in my hands. *I'm still fucking alive.*

Bang! Bang! Bang! Shit, maybe that's what woke me up. Someone's at the damn door. I throw back the sheet and step out of my bed. I pull my bedroom door open, and when I feel a cool breeze against my waist, remember I'm naked. *Shit.* I turn back quickly and throw a pair of loose sweats over my ass and reach the door as someone bangs on it again.

"Keep your fucking pants on!" I shout, pulling the door open, then cringe when I see who it is. *Fuck. Actually, she can take her pants, skirt, slacks, whatever the hell she wants off.* I lean against the door and lift one side of my mouth in a cocky grin to try to mask my surprise. "Doc. What brings you to my door?"

"Are you okay? I thought I heard you yell." Her brow creases in a cute little wrinkle right between her ice blue eyes as she looks up at me.

"I'm right as rain," I lie. I do that a lot to her. "Wanna come in?" I push off the door and wave my arm across the threshold in invitation.

"Um—" She stares at my bare chest for a minute, her eyes wide. "Well, I just wanted to drop this off." I glance down and realize she's probably shocked by the slash marks still healing on my skin. I look back up at her, but before I can say anything, she reaches into an oversized purse to pull out my jacket and then holds it out to me.

I look down at the jacket then back at her and nod. "You didn't have to do that." I turn, without taking the jacket from her, and walk into the apartment. I'm forcing her to follow me, just because she seems so damn uncomfortable, and I love having her in that position for once. "Come in."

"Um—" she stammers out again but then darts inside before the door can shut on her. "I'll just leave this on the couch."

"Can I get you a cup of coffee?" I start toward the kitchen, hearing soft whimpers coming out from under the bathroom door. "Shit!"

"What?" She picks up her pace, now just a few feet behind me. "What's wrong?"

"The puppy." I open the bathroom door, and the damn ball of fur comes bounding out, practically tripping over its own big paws. "It was crying all night, so I finally put it in there a couple hours ago so I could get some sleep."

She bends down, an enormous smile brightening her face, and scoops the puppy up into her arms. "Oh my gosh!" She starts cooing to it. "Aren't you just the cutest little thing on four legs?" The puppy starts lapping at her face, which only causes her smile to grow wider as she laughs out loud. "Are you hungry, little fella?"

She rises, cuddling the puppy up against her chest, still cooing at it, and walks closer to me. "He's adorable! I would have never guessed you were a puppy kind of guy."

I cross my arms and snarl my response. "I'm not."

"He's not yours?"

"Well, kind of." I uncross my arms and walk behind the kitchen counter to make some coffee. "My old roommate's fiancée gave him to me yesterday. Thought he would be good for me."

"Hmm. She might be right." She lifts the puppy, turning

its face to hers, and gives it a kiss on the nose. Is it wrong to be jealous of a puppy?

"Just what the doctor ordered?" My tone is filled with sarcasm, which earns me an eye roll from her.

"What's his name?" She puts him down and laughs out loud when he starts chasing his tail round and round. I watch, smiling when the dopey little thing falls over dizzy.

"Puppy?" I shrug my shoulders. "I'm only keeping him a week. I told her I'd give it a try." I watch as it gets up, finds the little stuffed toy he's become attached to, and begins chewing on it. "He's going to turn into a damn candy cane if he keeps that up." I motion to the dog then scratch my chin in thought. "Hey, there's an idea."

She glances up from the puppy. "What's an idea?"

"How about Kane for a name?"

She looks down at the puppy again, connecting the dots to the candy cane reference, and then back at me, her face beaming. "Yes! I like it!"

"There, he has a name then." I cross my arms. "Happy?"

She walks closer, placing her hands flat on the counter before facing off against me again. "Still going to get rid of him in one week?"

This time, it's her tone that's laced with sarcasm. I pull the freshly brewed cup of coffee out of the Keurig and place it on the counter in front of her. "You want cream or sugar?" Even though there's a thick slab of granite between us, I can tell I make her uneasy when she takes a small step back.

"I'm not staying." She takes another step back, her bottom lip now locked between her teeth, her gaze fixed on my naked chest again.

I glance down to see where she's looking and chuckle when I realize it's my piercing. I look back up, and unable to help myself, brush a hand over my pec, running my fingers deliberately over my nipple. "You should stay."

Her eyes grow a little wider, and she almost stumbles over the puppy as she tries to retreat. "No, I should go. I have a patient." She turns abruptly and grabs her large bag off my couch, swinging it over her shoulder as she scurries to the door, yanking on the handle twice before getting it open. "I'll see you at our appointment on Friday."

Before I can even reply, the door slams shut behind her. I let out a long breath, adjust my raging cock, and smile as I take a sip of the coffee.

CHAPTER FIVE

~Annabelle~

"I can't believe I let you talk me into this," I state for at least the fourth time in the last half-hour as I look at myself in the mirror. "I don't even know who that is." I point at my reflection and then turn to look at Holly.

"Isn't it fun though? Being someone else for a little while?" She giggles and leans into the mirror, adjusting one of the lashes adhered to her darkly colored lids.

I look at myself again and just stare. My usually long, wavy chestnut hair has been securely hidden under a golden blonde, shoulder-length shag bob, making me look different enough, but it's my eyes I'm transfixed upon. My light blue irises are now a tawny brown, surrounded by long full lashes, painted thick with mascara. Something I rarely wear. Combined with the rich red lipstick and nails, I feel like a complete imposter in this disguise. But not unpretty. No, I actually feel very attractive.

Holly found a short black satin negligee in my drawer that she found acceptable, but made me pair it with a garter and silk stockings. I wanted to wear my black satin pumps, but she insisted I wear my knee-high patent leather boots instead. I only ever wear these boots under long skirts, so pairing them with a barely-there skirt felt so awkward but also very sexy.

"Okay, put this on." She hands me a long black trench coat. I slide it on, tying the belt around my waist extra tight, my hands shaking slightly. "And don't forget this." She hands me a little black purse with a shoulder chain. Just big enough to hold my phone, credit cards, and some lipstick. She's dressed in a tight red corset, black leather short-shorts, and over the knee tie-up boots with big, clunky heels. She puts on a coat as well and then ushers me out of my apartment and down to a waiting Uber.

Twenty minutes later, we're standing in the lobby of a really nice building, waiting in line, our coats checked. Ten minutes later, I'm filling out paperwork with my name and signing away any liability to the club, agreeing to the 'rules' laid out in the form. I scan them quickly and sign. I'll only be watching, so I don't get caught up in the fine print. Five minutes after that, Holly and I are led to an elevator, up five flights—*why did I think we'd literally be in a basement*—and then into a beautifully decorated lounge area.

"See, this isn't so bad, right?" Holly links her arm with mine and whispers.

I scan the room and agree. The room is tastefully decorated in dark purple, red, and black velvets. Soft couches circumference the room, with tables and soft-cushioned chairs throughout the open area between. There is a large bar at each end of the room, each lined with padded stools. I beeline for a stool at the bar on the far end of the room and pull Holly with me.

"Let's just sit here and have a drink first, okay?" I suggest, sliding myself as elegantly as I can onto the stool, hoping I'm not exposing my nether regions to half the room.

Holly reaches over and squeezes my hand. "Of course." She slides onto the stool next to me and signals the bartender, requesting two glasses of champagne. When he returns, she slides one bubbling flute next to me. "Drink this. It will help you to relax."

"I'm relaxed," I shoot back, bringing the glass to my lips to take a large sip.

"Uh-huh." She looks over at me, smiles, and then winks. "Remember, you don't have to do anything you don't want to do. And if you do, no one will ever know who you are."

"Easy for you to say, Miss Dungeons and Dragons over there." I giggle and take another sip of my drink, scanning the room over the rim of my glass, almost choking when I lock eyes with a pair almost directly across the room at the other bar. I spin my stool around, turning my back to the room, and hiss out to Holly, "Oh my God, oh my God, oh my God!"

"Are you having an orgasm, or are you trying to tell me something?" She spins around as well and leans closer to me.

"He's here!" I seethe out between clenched teeth.

"Patrick?" She spins around again, glancing around the room.

"Don't look for him, Holly!" I grab her arm and turn her back to me. "Make it obvious, why don't you?"

"So what?" She cups a hand over mine. "Belle, I'm telling you, he will never know it's you in this disguise. You're totally safe. And there are thirty other women in here. I'm sure he's not going to single you out."

"Hello, ladies." A strong, dark voice interrupts our conversation. We straighten in our stools and both twist at the same time. I audibly sigh in relief when it's not Patrick. We both nod and say hello. He's an extremely handsome gentleman, dressed in slacks and a white button down, an expensive watch on his wrist.

"I was wondering if you came as a pair?"

It hits me right then. Right there. I'm in a fucking sex club. Yes, the pun is intended. *Holy shit. What did I get myself into*? I turn to look at Holly, praying she'll handle this, which of course, she does. She practically purrs a response to him. "Unfortunately, for us I think, we do not."

"Perhaps another time then?" He takes Holly's hand and places a kiss to the back of her knuckles then leaves us both with a nod.

"Did that just happen?" I turn and hold my hand over my mouth as I try to contain the nervous laughter trying to escape.

"Would you be okay here for a little while on your own?" She turns her head in the direction of a man dressed in faded jeans and a tight black t-shirt sitting on one of the couches. "I think I'd like to get me a piece of that."

I laugh at her boldness and nod my head. "Go. I'll be fine." I wave as she steps off the stool, and then growl playfully after her. "Go get him!"

She walks up to him, sits beside him, and begins to speak. I watch them for a minute but soon find my eyes wandering across the room to where Patrick was standing before. He's not there, so I scan the room, my heart skipping a beat when I find him. He's sitting at one of the tables, not quite as far away from me now, drinking some kind of dark liquid from a tumbler. He's not looking at me this time, so I take in this different side of him, so unlike what I've seen in my office. He's dressed nicely. Very nicely, in fact. Designer slacks and a fitted black button up shirt. His hair is actually brushed, and his face is free of stubble.

"Is this seat taken?" I swing my attention to the person speaking next to me and stare for a moment.

"Oh, no." I point to the chair. "Please."

"Thank you."

I watch as he makes himself comfortable and then orders a scotch from the bartender. "Would you like another champagne?" he asks me, looking at my nearly empty glass.

I look at my glass, then him, and shake my head. "Not right now, thank you."

"Are you looking for a demonstration of anything in particular? I'd be happy to help." He smiles, scattering goosebumps across my flesh, and not the good kind.

"Not right now, thank you again."

"Certainly." He stands with his scotch and holds out his hand. "I'm Anthony, if you change your mind."

I put my hand in his, but instead of shaking it, he lifts it and kisses my fingers before releasing them and walking away. Is this a thing here? This kissing thing? I look down at my fingers and almost grimace. Before I can even recover from Anthony's request, someone else is sliding into the stool next to me. I'm relieved when I look over and it's a woman. Unfortunately, my relief doesn't last long.

"You're very beautiful." She reaches over and strokes my hair, then frowns. "It's a wig?"

"Yes." I nod, and smile.

"It's a good one. I wouldn't have known if I hadn't touched it." She looks me over then, scanning me from head to toe, then finds my eyes again. "I'd love to taste you. Find out what color your hair really is." Her gaze falls between my legs. "Are you bare?"

Holy shit. I definitely haven't had enough to drink for this. I smile. "I'm sorry, you're quite attractive but not my type."

She scoffs then poufs up her hair. "You don't like brunettes?"

"I don't like pussy."

"Touché." She laughs out loud. "You told me, didn't you?" She motions to the bartender. "Buy this one another glass of champagne, please, Paul, and put it on my tab." She turns back to me, rises off the stool, smiling. "I like you. You've got fire." She gives me a small finger wave. "See you around, Blondie."

I can't help the smile my lips form as she saunters away,

and I happily accept the champagne she's ordered me, knowing there are no strings attached. I take a small sip, the glass frozen against my lips when I hear a voice I recognize beside me. "I've been watching you."

Turning my head to the side, I lock eyes with cool green ones that I know well, my heart lodging in my throat.

CHAPTER SIX

~Trick~

I hate demo nights at The Den. Dealing with wanna-be submissives and curious housewives who've read that one famous book way too many times and think they're going to find what they need in a place like this. But it's part of my contract as a member here, and particularly, as a trained member of the club, to participate in these events at least twice a year.

So, here I am, bored out of my fucking mind, hoping against hope no one approaches me for a demonstration. Until, that is, the woman across the bar locks eyes with me, sending a shiver down my spine. I feel like I know her, but I can't place her or her friend in any of my memories. I mean, let's face it, I've fucked a shit ton of women over the last few years. Some here, some through my work at Temptations, but I can't remember ever having her as a client either.

"Hey, handsome, you want a drink?" Samantha, the bartender working, and also one of my more frequent fucks here at The Den, asks from behind me.

"Sure, Sam. I'll have a bourbon. Bulleit, straight-up." I turn back to the bar, noticing the blonde being approached by one of our more prestigious Doms, Michael, and focus my attention on the drink I'm handed a moment later.

"Heard you took quite the beating from Mistress Blue the other night." Sam reaches her hand across the bar and drags her long, claw-like nails down the back of my hand.

My eyes follow the path of her nails and then trail slowly up her body until I'm looking in her eyes. "Guess nothing's a secret around here these days."

"I can keep a secret," she mewls out. "I bet I can make you feel so much better than she did."

"I bet you can." I take a sip of my drink, the liquid warm as it flows through my blood, thawing away some of the coldness within.

"You know where to find me." Her tongue darts out and swipes across her lips seductively, a smile at the very edges forming, before she turns her attentions away from me and waits on someone further down the bar.

I unbutton the cuffs on my shirt then roll up each sleeve to mid-way on my forearms, glancing at my watch. Jesus, it's only nine-thirty. It's going to be a long night. I take my drink off the bar, turning as I take a sip, surprised to see the blonde is still sitting in the same spot with her friend. Not very many people say no to Michael. Not only is he exceptionally good looking, he's extremely rich. Interesting.

Deciding to move away from the bar, and Samantha, I

move a little closer to my mystery woman. I want to get a better look, to see if I can remember where I know her from. I find a table that has a clear view of her and sit, watching as I sip on my drink. Her friend leaves her to go talk to a man, and I can't help but wonder if she'll leave. She seems nervous, but she stays put, approached almost immediately by Anthony. Fucking pussy. I can't stand him. He pretends to be nice to a girl then rips her to shreds as soon as he has her alone and in his clutches. I'm still not quite sure how he hasn't been thrown out yet.

I'm relieved when I see her rebuff his attentions, too. Yes, this is very interesting. What in the world is she doing here if she isn't going to say yes to anyone, nor approach anyone herself? I think my question's going to be answered when I see Pamela sit beside her and begin to have an actual conversation with her. Gay? But I'm surprised again when I see Pamela get up and walk away.

Without even thinking about it, I decide I'm going to figure out what she wants. I am out of my chair, headed her way before I can second-guess my own actions. Her back is to me, so she doesn't see when I approach and slide quietly onto the stool next to her. "I've been watching you."

She turns her head, and I find myself staring at wide caramel colored eyes. *Why was I expecting blue eyes?* "I'm sorry, what?"

Her voice is soft and whispery, and also familiar, but I can't recall from where. "Have we met before? You look so familiar."

"No, I don't think so," she says quietly, fiddling with the stem of her glass, then looks back at me. "I'm Belle."

I search my memory for a Belle but come up blank. I reach my hand out to shake hers, but she moves to get up. "I was actually just leaving."

I place my hand over her arm and push her gently back down. "But you haven't found what you came for yet."

She sits back in the seat and analyzes me for a moment before replying. "What do you mean? I wasn't looking for anything."

"I've been watching you," I repeat.

"So you said," she bites out.

"Three times you were approached, and three times you said no."

"So?"

One side of my mouth cocks up in confidence. "That means one of two things. You're either afraid, or you didn't find what you were looking for."

She stares at me for a long moment before responding, her voice barely above a whisper. "Can't it be both?"

My brows shoot up in surprise. I wasn't expecting her to admit that. I lean closer and take one of her hands in mine, stroking my fingers softly across the inside of her wrist. "Yes, it can be both. Why don't you tell me what you're looking for, and I'll see if perhaps I can't make you feel less afraid."

She presses her lips together firmly and pulls her hand out of my grasp, shaking her head back and forth. "I think maybe I should go, that maybe I made a mistake."

I turn her stool so her legs are between mine and place both of my hands on the arms of her stool, caging her in, then speak again. "You've come this far. Tell me. Maybe I can help."

She peeks up at me under dark, heavy lashes, her cheeks pinking before finally speaking in a rush. "I want to know how someone gets pleasure from pain."

Her statement jars me, my body physically leaning back from her in response. This is a question I've heard before, and it's also an answer I know I can provide. I feel my cock stir between my legs as I rake my eyes down her body. "You want someone to hurt you?"

She shakes her head back and forth, pulling her shiny, red lower lip between her teeth. "I want to know how it can bring you pleasure."

I sit back, pondering her question. The kind of pain I like is different. I feel I deserve to be punished. I need to be punished to stave away the pain I feel in my bones every day over the loss of my crew, for not being able to help them. Wanting pain, purely for the pleasure of it, is something different, but something I know how to provide. Just not how to receive.

"I can help you." I lean close to her again and lower my voice. "Do you want me to show you?"

Her eyes lock with mine, and she slowly bobs her head up and down.

"I need to hear you say, yes. It's not enough for you to just nod your head."

She nods again, but this time speaks in her hushed voice, "Yes, I want you to show me."

Fuck, my dick just got hard as a rock. "Come with me." I stand, take her hand, and pull her through the crowd to a doorway leading to the private rooms. I walk quickly, stopping at a door with a green light above it, pushing through, and pull her in with me. I shut the door and turn the lock, knowing this will switch the light to red, indicting the room is in use.

I turn and see her eyes canvasing the room, taking in the large bed, the cross on the wall, the chains, ropes, canes, whips, and the large chest of drawers against another wall. Her hands are clenched in front of her, her feet shuffling back and forth.

"Are you scared?"

Her eyes dart from the cross on the wall to me. "Yes."

I'm about to tell her not to be when she continues. "But I'm excited, too."

Fuck me. I want to throw her up against the wall and slam my dick into her until she screams my name. But this isn't about me. And, suddenly, I'm so glad I came to demonstration night after all. I walk over to the bed and sit on the end of it. "Come here."

She hesitates for a second but then walks over.

"Sit." I pat the spot next to me. She sits, obeying me again. She's more submissive than she realizes.

"I need you to know that I'm not going to hurt you, that I'm not going to do anything unless I think it will bring you pleasure. Okay?"

She looks at me with her soft brown eyes and nods. "Okay."

"But we still need to have a safe word. You know what that is, right?"

She nods again. "Yes, I say it if I want you to stop. Stop doesn't really mean stop in one of these places."

I chuckle. "Yes, I guess that's true. Do you have a word you want to use?"

"Um, Oreo?" she suggests.

"Oreo?" I question.

"It's the least sexual thing I can think of off the top of my head," she explains.

"Oreo it is."

"Can I ask you something?" she asks quietly, fiddling with her nail polish.

"Of course. Anything."

"What should I call you? Master or sir?"

I realize that I never had a chance to tell her my name because I was so intent on getting her not to leave. "My name is Trick, which is fine, unless we're in a scene. Then I'm your master and you can call me sir."

"Okay." She continues to fidget with her fingers.

"Belle, have you ever been tied up?"

Her head whips in my direction, her eyes wide. "No."

"Spanked or whipped?" I watch as her eyes grow wider.

"No." She's back to whispering again.

"But you want to know how some pain can be pleasurable? I can try to show you, but you have to be willing. I won't force you."

She nods her head slowly. "Yes, I want to know."

My cock twitches at her fear and eagerness rolled into one, her complete and utter innocence of this world, and her curiosity about it. "Can you tell me why?"

She's silent for a long time but finally answers. "Because nothing else I've done with a man feels good. Or right. Or turns me on. The men I've been with have never even gotten me off. Just thinking about you doing this to me makes me excited."

"Good, that's a good answer." I stand then, pulling her up with me, and before she can question what's next, I wrap a hand around her head and pull her lips against mine in a kiss. She gasps at the first touch, stiffening, but as I pull her against my body, I feel her relax. Her hands find my arms and trail up their length, one reaching up to grasp the nape of my neck. I deepen the kiss, sweeping my tongue across her lips, forcing them open, her tongue waiting for mine.

She lets out a moan and presses her body flush against mine, her hand gripping my bicep so tightly I can feel her nails digging into my skin. I tear my mouth from hers and trail wet kisses down her throat, over her chest, and over the silk material of her top, clamping down on her peaked nipple through the fabric. She lifts a leg and tries to wrap it around me as I suck hard, her back arching into me, her hand reaching down to rub over my throbbing cock. *How in the world did she think she wasn't responsive? I've never felt someone be so fucking responsive.*

I release her nipple and push her away roughly. She whimpers and looks up at me like a lost child. "What?"

"You're not nervous anymore, right?"

She nods, biting her lip.

"Then you're ready."

"Okay." She takes a small step back. "What are you going to do? Are you going to whip me?" She stares in the direction of the wall where numerous types of whips and canes are hanging.

I smile and move closer to her, taking her hand. "No, of

course not. You're not anywhere near ready for something like that. But I am going to spank you."

"Oh!" A breathy exclamation leaves her round mouth.

"And I think you're going to like it," I drawl out, pushing her down onto the bed so she's sitting, and then kneel at her feet. "But first, I'm going to take these boots off. These heels could do way more damage to me than I could ever do to you if you decided to rear back and kick me like a horse."

She laughs and then nods in understanding. I kneel at her feet, grip onto the heel of the first boot, and pull, sliding it easily off her foot. I do the same with the other boot, setting it down beside the first one I removed. I lift her tiny feet and can't resist running my hands up the smooth, sheer silk covering her leg, bringing my mouth down to kiss the top of her foot, then freeze. *Holy fucking hell.* My eyes lock onto the small rose with one falling petal tattooed right above her ankle. My heart starts to pound so loud I can feel the blood whooshing in my ears.

This cannot be a coincidence. This tattoo is too unique. But the blonde hair and the brown eyes? I lower her foot and raise my eyes up to hers. I notice then that she's wearing contacts that spin just slightly off center when she blinks, revealing a hint of blue. It really is her. *This is Doctor fucking Murphy.* It has to be. And she has no fucking clue that I know.

CHAPTER SEVEN

~Annabelle~

Oh my god. I can't believe Patrick Connors, my patient, just took my damn boots off and is kneeling at my feet. I know without a doubt this is wrong. On so many levels. But I can't deny how much I want him, and how much I want him to do this to me. Every single nerve in my body is tingling with desire, a feeling so foreign to me and one I didn't realize I was craving. Until now. Until he brought me into this room and I saw what could be delivered here.

I shiver as his fingers skim down my leg, even though I feel like my blood is boiling beneath my skin. My eyes lock onto his as he lowers my foot, a darkness I haven't seen before staring back at me. He squints as he continues to gaze at me, the hand around my foot squeezing tightly. Before I can react, he releases his grip and stands, his features hardening as he looms over me. His hand darts out and latches onto my wrist, pulling to lift me off the bed until I'm standing next to him.

He releases his hold on my wrist and places a finger under my chin, raising it until I'm looking straight at him. He analyzes me for what seems like an eternity then finally speaks, his tone gruffer than before. "Are you sure this is what you want?"

"Yes." I don't even hesitate in my response.

"Then let's get started." He releases the hold on my chin. "We only get thirty minutes to provide a demonstration to someone who isn't a member of the club."

"Oh." I frown, not entirely sure why this time limit bothers me. "Okay."

He chuckles, one side of his mouth quirking up as if he can read my mind. "It's enough time, don't worry." Then he moves to sit on the bed. "Come."

He extends his hand, and I place mine within. His fingers tighten around mine right before he yanks my body toward his, pushing me down over his lap in one quick motion. A small yelp falls from my lips when my chest meets his thighs, my free hand flying to my head to insure my wig stays in place.

"Give me your hand." His voice is low, but the tone is commanding and one I know instinctively not to challenge. I immediately release the hold I have on my hair, thankful the wig stayed firmly in place, and hold it out in front of me. He takes my other hand and joins them together, stretching them out in front of me, placing them on the bed. "Leave them there. Understand?"

I nod, speaking quickly, my breathing matching my

erratic pulse. “Okay.” I hear the slap before I feel it, just a slight stinging, but my whole body convulses at the shock.

“You’ll answer yes sir or no sir from now on.” I feel his chest press against my back as his lips brush against my ear, hot breath drowning out any other sounds. “Understood?”

“Yes, sir,” I rush out.

“Good girl.” He lays his palm slowly against the area on my bum he just slapped and caresses it, a hum vibrating from his chest. “I think these need to go.” His fingers glide higher to the waist band of my panties and begin bunching the material before pulling them down, exposing my entire backside.

I twist my head to look at him, my body lifting at the same time, but still when I see the expression on his face. His hand flattens on my lower back, pushing my waist back into his lap. “Are you quitting already?” He cocks his head. “Just use your safe word and I’ll let you up.”

I release the grip my teeth have on my lower lip to reply huskily, “No, sir.”

His lips curve up into a tight smile as he nods. “I’m going to spank you six times. Count, or I’ll add more.”

“Okay,” I gasp out.

His brows rise as his smile grows wider, and I realize my mistake too late as I feel his hand smack against my tender flesh.

“Ow!” My heels kick up at the contact. “I mean, yes, sir!”

“Count,” he growls out.

“One!” I spit out.

“That’s better.” He places his hand over the spot throbbing on my ass and begins rubbing it in a small circle, lessening the pain pulsing against my skin, shifting and spreading it thin. He does this for only a minute before lifting his hand and bringing it down again, this time on the other side of my ass but just as hard.

"Two," I squeak out between clenched teeth. So far, this just hurts. I don't understand how it's supposed to feel good. But then, he begins the soft, circular motion with his hand again, the heat moving lower, igniting a tingling sensation between my legs. I squirm, trying to tighten my legs in an effort to quell the feeling.

He chuckles, his weight on my back, lips tickling the edge of my earlobe again. "You like it."

I'm not sure why, but shame floods through me as I answer hoarsely. "Yes, sir."

He groans and I feel his length jerk, hard and thick against my side. Before I can react, his hand comes down again, a little harder, a little lower, hitting me evenly across both cheeks. A low moan leaves my mouth, my pelvis thrusting against his leg, before I manage to say three. The massaging, even lower this time, only fuels the heat building in my core.

His hand lifts again, but this time, he slaps me twice in a row, once on each side of my buttocks, hard and fast. I'm so surprised, I almost forget to count, but spit out, "Four! Five!" before he can punish me further. His fingers brush over my skin, so sensitive now, his light touch causing the flesh across my body to erupt in goosebumps. My hands clench the bed covering, the material balled in my fingers, in an effort to try to keep my body still as I feel my pussy contract and flood with heat. I want to sit up and straddle him, push myself up and down on his cock until I come.

His fingers skim so low, almost brushing against my swollen lips, and my ass pushes back, inviting him to please, please go lower. I feel his body vibrate again, and I almost rise up to confront him but stop when he begins to speak in a hushed voice. "Do you know why they say this feels so good to some people? Why getting spanked, or giving yourself totally over to someone else is so pleasurable?"

I'm a doctor of psychiatry. I'm not stupid by any means, and I obviously understand that, for some, pain equals pleasure. But it isn't something I have ever entertained or thought about until recently. I don't need pain to feel good. Or do I? "I don't know," I murmur, my emotions speaking instead of my brain.

His lips graze against my ear again. "You mean, no, sir?" His hand stills on my ass, and I flinch, waiting for another blow. Instead, he runs his nose against my cheek and pulls back. "It's about the control."

"What?" My brow wrinkles as I turn to look at him.

"People who live their lives in complete control, or in control of others. In coming here, they can give that up, let someone else have all that, all the decisions, all the power, for just a little while. It's a relief. A weight lifted."

I think about what he's said and am about to respond when he continues. "Is that your problem, Belle?" His hand is back on my ass, caressing it again, but all I notice is how sharply he enunciated my name, almost in anger. "Do you have too much control in your life?"

"I don't—" I start to defend myself but am silenced when his hand strikes me a final time, this time so low he brushes the very edge of my pussy. "Six!" I mewl out as his hand immediately begins rubbing my ass in a slow, circular motion, my grip on the covers deadly. I can't stop myself when I raise my hips and press my ass more firmly against his hand. I want more. The stinging sensation has traveled straight to my pussy, causing it to throb with need.

"Let's see, shall we, Belle?" My name is punctuated again as he speaks roughly. "Let's see if this answered your question." He slides his hand between my ass cheeks and follows it all the way down until his fingers skim against my pussy. He groans out loud when he drags them harder against my opening, this time pushing two fingers inside of me, my wet core pulsing tightly around him. "Did you find pleasure in the pain?"

"Yes," I admit and shove myself against his hand, whimpering in relief as I feel myself grip onto him, any shame I felt overridden by desire. Before I can surge myself even further, he pulls his hand free from between my legs and moves to shift me off his lap in one fell swoop.

I cry out, my hands clutching for the surface of the bed as I try to regain my balance. He stands and glares down at me. I look up at him, wide-eyed and confused. "What's wrong? What did I do wrong?"

He looms over me, his eyes dark, his mouth in a firm line, his hands fisted at his sides. I stand, my fingers finding the hem of my negligee, pulling it lower in an attempt to cover more of myself than possible with the short material. I repeat my question when he doesn't answer me. "Did I do something wrong?"

He blows out a breath as he crosses his arms, hands still

clenched, and looks up at the ceiling then shakes his head. "No."

I bend down while he's looking away and snake my panties off the floor to slide them back on. When I complete my task, I look up to find him staring at me again. "Then why do you seem angry at me?"

"I'm not." He uncrosses his arms and points to a door. "That's a bathroom. You can clean up or do whatever you need to do in there. There's ibuprofen for the pain."

"Okay," I say cautiously and look in the direction he pointed. "Is that all?"

He shrugs dismissively. "It's a demonstration. You had a question, and I'm pretty sure I answered it for you."

I cock my head and look at him, my mouth hanging open slightly as I try to figure out how things went from really hot to really cold. But then, this is Patrick Connors I'm dealing with. Emotions aren't something he deals with on a regular basis, so why should I expect them here in a sex club? "So, that's it? We're done?"

He nods. "If you're interested in joining the club, they have a thirty-day trial membership you can purchase when you leave."

I blink rapidly, trying to keep my stupid emotions in check, and nod once. "Well, all right then." I bend down to retrieve one of my boots and thrust my foot angrily into it, then look up at him. "I guess we are done."

His gaze drifts down my body then trails back up to lock onto my eyes before he finally speaks again, desire in his voice. "I'm here almost every weeknight if you want to see me again."

I scoff, shoving my other foot into my boot, then stand abruptly, no longer intimidated by him. "You're serious?"

"You're angry." He reaches out and takes each of my forearms in a light grip, stepping closer to me, drawing our bodies flush. He latches his gaze onto mine, lowering his head until his lips brush lightly against my open mouth. "Don't be," he whispers as he leans even closer, my eyes closing as a new wave of longing sweeps over me. "I'd love to explore more of you, see what else your body craves." He sweeps another soft kiss against my lips, on my cheek, and then against the base of my ear. His breath is hot as he exhales and then whispers, "But time's up."

My eyes snap open at his words, but all I see is his back as he strolls out of the room, a low chuckle left in his wake as the door closes. *Holy shit, please tell me that was a coincidence.*

CHAPTER EIGHT

~Trick~

It's been less than twelve hours since I left her in that room in The Den, and here I am, standing outside the door to her office, staring at the nameplate attached, wondering what the fuck the A stands for.

A. Murphy
Doctor of Psychiatry

The first and only invoice I received from her office so far also just had her first initial. She called herself Belle last night. Did she just make up a name? I lift my hand to knock but then lower it as I take a step back. I hope I didn't push my luck too far last night when I left.

Every single session I've ever had with her, I've fled, always citing, "Time's up" as my get out of jail free card. But there was that small part of me last night, the evil part, that wanted to leave her wondering. That shit is clearly backfiring on me now. I'm the one left standing here, hesitant to enter her office, wondering if she knows. Does she know that I know she liked the pain? That she wanted me. Does she know now that there is a side to her that I don't think she even realized was lurking in her. What she doesn't know is that I want her just as much.

"Fuck it," I mumble. If I'm going to make her squirm, I'm going to have fun doing it. Without knocking, I push through the door, startling her when I breeze in. "What's up, Doc?"

"Patrick." She rises from behind her desk, glancing at the clock on the wall. "You're early."

"Am I?" I shrug out of my jacket, the same one she returned to me earlier this week, and hang it on the rack beside the door. I turn and look at her, strolling over to the same chair I sit in every visit, and plop myself down. "There's a first for everything, I guess." I cock one side of my mouth up in a grin, my sentence serving a dual purpose, even if she's not aware of that.

She doesn't take the bait. Instead, she grabs a notepad off her desk and moves to sit on the couch across from me. I scan her body discreetly, knowing so much more about it than I did just one day ago. I can't help but be a little disappointed when I see she's dressed more conservatively than usual, in dark wool slacks and an ice blue cashmere turtleneck. Her feet and ankles are effectively hidden in fitted boots. I was so hoping for another look at her tattoo. I wanted to see it again, to confirm it was indeed her across my lap last evening. Thinking about it causes my cock to stir, so I shift in the chair, crossing one of my ankles over my knee.

"I've been thinking, Patrick—" she starts, but before she can continue, I cut her off.

"What's your first name?"

She frowns, her lips pursing for a moment before replying. "What?"

I uncross my leg and lean forward. "I was just wondering what your first name is."

"Why?" She blinks rapidly, her body visibly tensing.

"Well, you know my full name." I lean back, clasping my hands behind my head, stretching my chest, watching as her eyes follow my movements. "Isn't it only fair that I know yours?"

One corner of her mouth pulls down, and the crinkle between her eyes that I've come to adore appears. "These sessions aren't about me. They're about you."

I scoff, lowering my arms to rest on the chair. "Is it some big fucking secret? I mean, I am paying you two hundred dollars a fucking hour. Is it really unheard of that I'd want to know the name of the person I'm giving my fucking money to?"

She stares at me for a moment, her mouth moving slightly as she clenches her teeth before speaking. "You're angry."

My brows rise. I used those same words against her last night. "No. Just curious."

"You just used the word fuck three times," she challenges.

"I like the word fuck." I lean forward again, lowering my voice when I continue. "It's a good word." I chuckle when she rears back against the couch. "And you still haven't answered my question." I smirk, continuing. "I thought evasion was my specialty."

Her knuckles turn white as she grips the pen in her hand and begins tapping it against the notepad on her lap, her knee bouncing in time with it. I've made her nervous. Good.

"Forget it," I toss out. "I didn't realize it was going to be such a big fucking thing."

She sighs. "I just think it's important to keep things professional. That's easier to do if we keep things formal."

Is she fucking kidding me? I had my fingers in her god damn pussy last night. It occurs to me then that she's not sure if I know that it was her last night. And she's not taking any chances. I nod, sneering out my response. "Whatever."

Neither of us say anything for several long seconds before her soft voice breaks the silence. "It's Anna." I lift my head and lock eyes with her. We stare at each other until she finally blinks her lids shut, turning her head to look at the clock. When she turns back to look at me, she seems to have regained her composure.

"Thank—"

"Patrick—"

We both begin speaking at the same time, and both stop. She fidgets with the pen in her hand, clears her throat, and starts again. "Patrick, I think it would be better if I assigned you to another colleague."

My eyes narrow, and my nostrils flare when I register what she's just said. I knew last night might make her uncomfortable, but I definitely wasn't expecting this response from her. "What the fuck for?" I stand, my jaw clenching.

"Please, sit down." She nods, pointing to the chair.

"I don't want to sit down." I widen my stance and cross my arms over my chest, prepared to stand my ground. "Why don't you want to be my doctor anymore?" I know exactly why she doesn't want to be my doctor anymore, but frankly, I'm surprised she would dismiss me so easily.

Since I don't sit, she rises and moves to lean against her desk. "I've been seeing you twice a week for over a month now, and I just don't think we're making progress. You come to these appointments and barely speak. When you do, it's not about anything related to your PTSD, and that's what we need to be working on for you."

I take a few steps closer to her. "So, what, you're just going to give up on me? After only a few visits?"

"This is our eleventh visit. We've had more than a few." She turns and reaches for a card on her desk and holds it out to me. "And I'm not giving up on you. Take this." I stare at the card but don't move. "This is my friend, Anthony Sparks. He's a brilliant therapist, and I think he'd be a better fit for you. I've already spoken to him, and he has agreed to take you on."

I take two more steps, now only six inches away from her, but still don't take the card. She sighs and lowers her hand.

"What if I don't want another doctor?"

She lifts her eyes to mine, a sad smile on her face. "I think it's for the best."

"Do you think I can't be saved?" I blurt out.

Her mouth gapes open and she grabs onto my bicep. "No." She shakes her head, looking up at me, concern on her face. "Of course not. Why would you even think that?"

"I feel like we've just started, and you're already throwing in the towel."

"Please, no." The grip on my arm tightens as she tries to make her point. "That's not it at all. I just—" She closes her eyes and looks away then back up at me. "I'm trying really hard to do the right thing for you. To make sure you have a doctor who can really help you."

"And that's not you," I counter.

"I just—" She lets out a long sigh, releasing my arm as she does, and steps back. "No. That's not me."

"Why don't you tell me the real reason?" I take a bold step forward, placing a hand on either side of her on the desk, and drop my gaze onto her startled ones.

"What?" She stammers, lifting her hands to push against my chest. I don't move.

"Tell me why." I lean even closer. "Tell me the real reason you don't want me in your office anymore, Doctor Murphy."

She pushes against me again, her hands flat and tiny on my chest, but I don't budge. "Patrick, you're scaring me."

"Am I?" I lower my head so it's a fraction from hers, so close I can feel the heat of her breath against mine as she pants softly. "Or are you excited?"

I lock my feral gaze onto her dilated pupils. "Is this the reason you can't have me as your patient anymore, Doc?" I take one hand off the desk and skim it down the side of her face. "If I lowered my hand, would I find your breasts peaked in excitement?"

Her eyes widen, her breaths quickening. "If I pushed myself against your body right now, would you stop me?" I lean myself against her hands and chuckle when there's no resistance. "Would you be shocked to know how hard my cock is? That all I want to do is push you back against this desk and fuck you?" Her teeth bite onto her lower lip, and unable to hold back any longer, I bend down and swipe my tongue over her mouth.

"Is this what you really want to be doing with me in this office, Anna?" I drop my hand back onto the desk and push my full body against hers, my hard length pressing against her center, a whimper escaping her. Surging forward, I crush my mouth against hers and kiss her, moaning at the taste of her when she opens to sweep her tongue against mine.

Her arms slide up and around my neck, wrapping tightly as our kiss intensifies. Her legs spread, and I thrust my pelvis against her center, my cock jerking in approval as it rubs against her core, warm even through the fabric of our clothing.

I lift my hand, weaving my fingers through her wavy, brown locks to grasp her head, deepening our kiss. I rock my length against the seam of her pants, her mouth releasing mine as a groan slips past her lips. I move my lips and trace a path across her cheek, finding her ear, and run my tongue around its, rim, her body shivering underneath me.

I whisper, like the devil I am, "Is this the reason, *Belle*?" Then I rise abruptly, stepping back and away, her mouth forming an O of surprise, her chest heaving as she moves to sit up.

Smirking, I shake my head and lean forward to snatch the card she tried to give me earlier, a gasp falling from her mouth. I make sure to brush against her as I back up, leaving her with a final message. "You know where to find me."

Then I turn, stroll to the door, grabbing my jacket this time, and close it behind me as I exit, leaving no doubt that I know exactly who she is *and* where she was last night.

CHAPTER NINE

~Annabelle~

My ass falls back onto my desk, darkness clouding the edges of my mind, making me dizzy as I try to keep myself from hyperventilating. I expel long, slow breaths from my lips, a thousand thoughts at once screaming in my head. *He knows. How does he know?* I was in costume. I didn't even recognize myself when I looked at my reflection last night. Was it my voice? Did he see the application I filled out? Is that why he asked what my first name is?

No longer feeling like I'm going to fall over, I fumble behind me until my hand lands on my phone. After typing in the passcode, my fingers sweep to my contacts and press on Holly's name. Glancing at the clock, I know it's early for her. She generally doesn't go into the salon until early afternoon on Fridays, and after last night, I have no idea what time she went to bed.

"Belle?" A groggy voice carries over the line.

"Can I come over? Are you alone?" I rush out.

"What time is it?" A yawning sound. "Aren't you at work?"

"I'm taking the rest of the day off. Holly… he knows," I state. "He just left my office."

"Holy crap on a cracker." Covers whoosh as I hear her stand. "Get your ass over here."

Twenty minutes later, after calling my service to request they cancel the remainder of my appointments for the day and hailing the first taxi I could, I'm standing in line at Starbucks a block from Holly's apartment. There's no way I'm going in without caffeine, especially after waking her up early. She's like a bear coming out of hibernation if she doesn't get enough sleep.

"Can I get two grande mocha lattes, one sugar each, skim milk please? Can you make those double shots as well?" I pull a twenty out of my wallet and hand it to the cashier.

"Name?" she asks, politely giving me my change.

"What?" I look up from my wallet, startled. *What's with that damn question today?* And then I remember; they write your name on the cup. Before I can even reply, a deep voice carries over my shoulder, directed at the clerk.

"Belle."

My heart lurches in my chest, my stomach churning as I slowly twist my head to look over my shoulder. *You have to be kidding me.* The rest of my body turns, my pulse thundering through my veins as I seethe. "Are you following me?"

He cocks his head, chuckling as he scratches at the

stubble on his chin. "I could ask you the same question." He leans in close and speaks low. "Miss me already?"

I take a deep breath. Big mistake. *Jesus, why does he have to smell so damn good?* I blow it back out, determined not to let him get the better of me, and force my lips into a smile. "I'm visiting a friend. She lives near here."

"Me too."

"You're visiting a friend?" One brow shoots high as I gaze up at him. "Isn't that convenient," I deadpan.

He rolls his eyes. "No, I live near here."

"Oh." I obviously know where he lives. I delivered his jacket the other day. I just never made the connection to how close it is to Holly's place.

"Miss, um, Belle is it?" the clerk calls meekly. "You can pick your order up down there." Her polite way of asking me to move along so she can take care of the next customer. I wave at the clerk that I've heard her and scurry across the length of the room, as far away from him as I can get. Of course, it takes him only a minute to place his order, and naturally, he swaggers in my direction.

He stops a foot beside me, clasping his hands behind his back, his stance wide and his back straight. I work with a lot of military personnel, and it occurs to me as I watch him how ingrained certain behaviors are to them. I swing my gaze up to meet his, which is, of course, trained on me. A shiver runs down my spine at the intensity in which his green irises are staring back at me. I wonder again, for the hundredth time in the last half hour, how did he know it was me? "Did you think I didn't know?"

I frown. *Did I say that out loud?* No, I know I didn't. My

face heats and I shift my eyes to my feet, embarrassed that I seem so transparent. Curiosity gets the better of me though, and I brave looking up at him again to ask softly, "How *did* you know?"

His eyes travel down the length of my body then slowly climb back up until they lock with mine again. He opens his mouth to speak, and I step closer, needing to know this.

"Belle! Two lattes," the barista calls from behind the counter.

Patrick's attention swivels to the barista, interrupting whatever he was about to tell me, then back at me. "Coffee's up." He points to the counter. "Better get it while it's hot."

"You're not going to tell me." Disappointment and then anger surge through me.

He gives me a lopsided grin, walking up to the counter to grab the coffee the other barista just called out for Trick, "Gotta run."

"I hate you," I spit out.

He stops short next to me, bending down 'til his face is inches from mine, amusement painting his features. "No, you don't." He grins wickedly. "And when you realize that, you know where to find me." Then he straightens, places one foot in front of the other, and strolls past me to the exit.

I stare dumbfounded after him, speechless. "Belle! Second call for Belle." I twist my head back to the counter, confusion swirling in my brain. I move forward on autopilot to grab both cups then exit the shop, walking in a daze until I get to Holly's. I press the buzzer to her apartment, and a second later the door lock releases.

I climb up the two flights to her floor, the door to her

apartment swinging wide as I approach. "You got Starbucks," she moans out gratefully. "Give me." She wiggles her fingers at me when I reach her, and I hand one over. See, ravenous bear like behavior.

"You aren't even going to believe this." I stride by her and walk straight to her couch, plunking down on it.

She follows behind, taking a loud sip of the latte and humming in approval before lowering herself a foot away from me. "Tell me everything."

"The costume didn't work." I throw a hand up in the air, my lips forming a grimace as I shake my head. "He knows it was me last night."

One side of her pursed mouth shoots up as she looks at me skeptically. "Not possible. I wouldn't even have known it was you if I didn't know it was you." She frowns at her comment and shrugs. "You know what I mean."

"Well, he knew." I take a sip of my coffee then place it on the table in front of me so I can pull my jacket off. I'm about to continue when the buzzer for the door sounds. I glance at Holly as she rises off the couch.

"I called reinforcements." She glides over to the buzzer and pushes it. There's only one other person in our little circle, so I know she means Krystal. "I figured you could use the extra support."

"She's not in class today?" Krystal is Holly's younger sister, in her final year at NYU getting her Master's.

"Nope. It's spring break week." She opens the door, and a second later, Krystal breezes in, concern etched on her face as she heads straight to me.

"Are you okay, Belle?" She sits right next to me and gives me a one-armed hug, then stops. "You got Starbucks?"

"I'm sorry, I didn't know you were coming." I grab my cup and hand it to her. "Take it. Seriously, my stomach is in knots."

She happily accepts my offering and doesn't hesitate bringing the cup to her mouth to take a large sip. When she's done, she focuses on me. Holly is now sitting in a chair across from us. "Okay, tell me all about the spanker."

My eyes fly to Holly. "You told her about the spanking?"

"Well, yeah." She lifts her shoulders then drops them. "I had to catch her up on what happened."

My hand comes up to cover my face as I try and hide my mortification. "Please, tell me you didn't tell anyone else, Holly," I mumble through my fingers.

"Of course not! You know this stays between us."

I lower my hand when I feel like my face isn't a glowing ember any longer, and face my friends. I tell them about my meeting with Patrick that morning, how I 'fired' him as a client, and how at the end of our meeting, he revealed he knew it was me at the club last night with his little name drop. I finish the story up with my surprise run-in with him at Starbucks.

"I guess what you need to figure out, Belle, is if you want to see him again," Krystal starts. "You're clearly attracted to each other, and since he's no longer a client, you aren't breaking any ethical boundaries anymore."

"I agree," Holly chimes in.

"I don't think you guys understand." I stand and begin pacing. "He likes to be beaten. 'Til he bleeds. He has major issues that we never even dealt with. This isn't a man I'm compatible with."

Holly holds a hand up to stop me. "Didn't you tell me last night that you liked getting spanked. That it turned you on more than anything ever has before?"

I glare at her. "Don't throw my words back at me, Holly." I continue pacing. "There is no way I'm letting myself get mixed up with him. I know too much about him. I just need to put this behind me and forget any of it ever happened."

"If you're sure that's what you want," Krystal adds.

"I am." I nod my head once in confirmation. "Patrick Connors is nothing but trouble, and that's the last thing I need in my life."

"Okay," Holly accepts. "You're the boss."

"Besides, I have the annual medical ball next week." I stare at both of them. "You guys can help me go shopping for a dress, and Holly, you can make me extra beautiful. The room will be full of eligible bachelors."

Krystal's eyes light up. "Yes, rich, bachelor doctors!"

I'm relieved when the topic finally moves away from Patrick and onto the topic of dresses and shoes. They're things I honestly couldn't care less about, but it's a distraction I know I need if I want to try to forget the way I felt when I stepped into that room with Trick the night before.

CHAPTER TEN

~Trick~

I've been sitting in this club every night for almost a week. Hoping she'll come. Hoping she'll give in to her desire. Hoping she gives in to me. It's Thursday, six days since I last saw her in the coffee shop. It might be time to admit defeat, but that's something I've never done easily. I even cancelled every appointment Cory had scheduled for me at Temptations this week. I don't need the damn money, and anyway, this is more important to me.

The only saving grace is that my dreams are now being invaded by her instead of flames and screams. If you can call that a grace. Thoughts of her torment me almost as much as the ghosts of my past. I want her more than anything I can ever remember wanting, and I know she wants me, too. I feel it in my bones—well, one in particular—every time we've been near each other. After seeing how she reacted in that room with me, I know she also needs me. She needs what I can give her. What no one else has shown her.

I take a large taste of the bourbon in my glass and shift in my chair. My cock is throbbing against the zipper of my pants just thinking about her. I need to do something about this, and I'm not sure I can wait any longer. I need to surrender to the reality that she hasn't come, nor does it look like she's going to. My eyes stray to the bar, to the stool that Samantha is currently residing on. I know she can provide what I need, even if she's not really who or what I want right now. As if she can sense me staring at her, she tilts her head and returns my gaze, a seductive smile lifting her lips. I nod my head, just slightly, but it's all the invitation she needs to slide off the stool and saunter over to me.

She sinks gracefully into the chair next to me then reaches across the table, taking the drink from my hand to bring it to her mouth. She sips slowly, her eyes closing as she swallows, a hum of appreciation vibrating from her throat. "You're drinking the good stuff tonight."

She places the drink back in front of me as I nod in reply. I don't really feel like small talk right now. "Looking for something better?" Her brow arches as one side of her mouth moves up suggestively.

I grip the glass, raise it to my lips slowly, and down the contents in one swallow, my eyes never leaving hers. The glass thumps against the coaster when I drop it back to the table, and I stand and extend my hand to hers. This doesn't require a conversation. This isn't about making her feel wanted or pretty. She rises and slips her hand into mine, following where I lead.

When we reach an available room, we enter and I shut and lock the door behind us. She drops my hand and leans against the door. "What do you need?"

I walk to the wall, scan the inventory available, and pull a two-foot cane off a hook. It has eight individual pieces of hard rattan that are tethered together by a leather band. When the hard wood hits your flesh, it expands, intensifying the pain and punishment provided by the person yielding it. As I turn to hand it to Samantha, eyes sparkling in pleasure, my cock throbs in approval.

"Get undressed," she commands, any warmth to her tone now gone. I pull my shirt over my head then bend to unlace my boots to remove them. I unbutton then slide off my jeans, my length springing up against my navel hard and ready. She watches me, her tongue sliding against her lips as her gaze locks below my waist. I stand straight and wait for her next order.

She moves to me instead, closing her fingers in a light grip around my cock, stroking it several times as she drags the cane down my thigh. Her hold tightens as she clenches my girth, her nails biting into my tender flesh. I hiss when she yanks down, forcing me to my knees. I swing my gaze up, wincing as I hear the whoosh of the cane before it connects with the skin on my back.

"Head down!" she barks.

I bend forward, placing my weight on my elbows in front of me, kneeling on all fours in front of her. My eyes lock onto the small pair of panties that just landed on the floor in front of me. She bends down, picks them up, and begins wadding them into a ball. She holds them in front of my face. "Open."

I dart my eyes up to hers. My hesitation results in another sweeping motion of her arm with the cane landing squarely between my shoulders, my mouth falling open as I groan. She uses this to her advantage, stuffing the material in my mouth as she leans in close to me. "You might as well get used to the taste of my pussy now."

Nodding in compliance, I keep my eyes glued to the carpet. "Crawl over to the bed and place your arms out flat against the mattress."

I do what she says, the dense material of the carpet digging into my knees, scraping them raw. I deserve this. I deserve this humiliation. I'm here and they aren't. It's the mantra I keep repeating in my head. I lay my arms out flat across the bed, my entire back naked and exposed for her.

She steps up beside me, and I feel her finger brushing across my shoulders. It takes me a second, but I realize she's tracing the letters of my tattoo. It's confirmed when she speaks again. "All pain is fleeting?" She snickers. "Let's test that theory, shall we?" Her finger stops and is replaced by the eight sharp tips of the cane. I feel her press her bodyweight forward, the sharp tips digging into my skin before she drags it heavily down the length of my back.

I arch into the bed, my fists clenching, and growl through the pain as the points sear through my flesh.

"Yes, I know that hurts," Samantha coos above me. "But doesn't it feel good?"

I moan through the material in my mouth, drool leaking over my lips and down my chin as I try to speak. "More."

"With pleasure," she purrs, and I groan in relief when the cane crashes against my lower back, sending lightning exploding across my flesh, any thoughts of her, of them, lost, my mind now consumed by the storm of pain she's providing.

I lose track of how many times she hits me, all coherent thoughts scattering to the wind with each blow she delivers. My body feels like it's humming from the vibrations of her efforts, my cock limp after coming several times, my mind temporarily free. My hands are no longer clenched but splayed out in front of me, relaxed and welcoming the pain.

The blows stop, and I hear the cane thump to the ground, Samantha panting above me. Her fingers reach in and pull the now soaked material of her panties from my mouth. "Get on your knees."

I lift my body, and she spreads her legs wide, balancing on her feet, in front of me on the bed. "Make me come," she demands, fisting my hair as she pushes my head between her legs. I inhale deeply as I'm lowered, her scent strong, her arousal obvious. I lose myself in the soft, wet folds, my fingers and tongue feasting on her offering until she screams out her relief. I fall limply to the floor, wishing it was Belle's taste on my lips instead of hers, the last thought before I pass out.

"What the hell is wrong with you?" Trey storms through my door, walks by me, smacks me across the forehead for good measure, and continues past me to my bedroom.

"What the fuck?" I throw the game remote on the table,

Kane jolting awake with a yelp beside me as it crashes against some empty beer bottles, and stand.

"It's Saturday, asshole," he yells from my bedroom.

"And?" I throw back, completely lost as to what the problem is.

He appears in the doorway of my bedroom, my Armani tux hanging from his hand. "Ball? Charlotte? Date?" He frowns. "Ring any bells?"

"Shit." Yep, I did tell him I would take Charlie to the ball in his place since he has to work tonight. "I forgot."

He carries the tux to the bathroom door and hangs it over the top. "Clearly." He enters the bathroom and turns the shower on. "She's been down there for over an hour getting ready with Gabby. If you stand up my very emotional, very pregnant fiancée, I'll kick your fucking ass."

"I'm not going to stand her up." I stroll to the bathroom, yanking my shirt over my head as I stalk past him. "I just forgot."

"Yeah, get your head out of your ass." He takes a sharp breath. "Jesus, Trick, really?"

I still and turn, returning the hard stare he's giving me. He motions to my back. "That has to stop."

I take a step closer to him, invading his space. "Don't tell me what to do with my fucking body."

"It's not good for you," he seethes back.

"And don't tell me what's good for me." I turn back around, slide my sweats off, and step into the hot water. "You don't have a fucking clue what's good for me."

We've had this discussion many times, and it always ends the same way. I don't know why he keeps trying. This is my fucking pain to deal with. Not his. "Tell Charlie I'll be down in thirty minutes."

I grab the shampoo off the shelf and watch through the dripping glass door as my friend shakes his head in defeat and leaves, the door slamming a minute later.

Even though I'm pissed, I shrug that off and feel worse that I forgot about this damn ball. Most of the staff at the hospital goes, and because Trey is a physician's assistant, and not one of the medical doctors, he has no choice but to work the E.R. shift this evening. Charlotte and her best friend Gabrielle are both registered nurses at the hospital as well, and there was no way in hell they were going to miss a chance to get dressed up for a ball. Enter me, hero of the day, and fill-in date for Charlie.

Normally, Charlie and Gabby would have just gone together, but Gabby has just started dating some cop, and he's going as her date. I can't wait to see how that turns out. Gabby breaks more rules than anyone I know, especially that taking money for sex one that she often does at her other job, an escort at Temptations.

I finish my shower and shave, because damn, when did I grow a fucking beard, and put my tux on. I run some gel through my hair, spray on a bit of cologne, and look at myself in the mirror. On the outside, I look like a pretty decent guy. I frown. Too bad I know what really lurks under this disguise…

CHAPTER ELEVEN

~Annabelle~

The driver of the car I hired for the evening extends his hand to help me out of the back seat. I kick my black heeled foot out from under the layers of blood red tulle surrounding me and step onto the sidewalk. When both feet are on the ground, the driver releases his hold, handing me a card. "Just call me when you're ready, Dr. Murphy."

I take the card and slide it into my small, black velvet clutch, thanking him. I turn and stride through the entrance of the hotel, a Sapphire Resort. After stopping to check my fur wrap, I follow the signs to the ballroom. Not that I really need to. There are others dressed in gowns and tuxedos all headed in the same general direction, so I simply follow the herd.

I'm not sure why, but I'm nervous. I attended this function last year, but since I was on the arm of my now very ex-boyfriend, I suppose the added sense of security was present. And while I'm sure I could have found a date, I honestly didn't mind going alone. I know, once I get inside, I'll find colleagues to chat with, and if I'm lucky, maybe a few handsome, eligible bachelors to twirl around the dance floor with.

There's a restroom right before the entrance to the ballroom, so I slip inside to do a final check of my makeup. I sweep a fresh coat of dark red lipstick over my mouth and fluff my hair. I spent three hours at Holly's salon today getting the works—waxing, manicure, pedicure, and of course, my hair. Because my dress is strapless, she curled my tresses, leaving them soft and wavy down my back. For fun, she threw in some red colored highlights to match the dark, blood red shade of my dress. And the dress. This dress is everything. The top is a fitted, velvet corset with gorgeous matching silk ribbon that crisscrosses up the back. The front has a sweetheart neckline that exposes just enough to be sexy but not so much that it's trashy. But the skirt, that is what I love. Layers and layers of soft, wispy tulle fall down to the floor, a short train flowing out behind me when I walk. I spin in a small circle before the mirror, smile once at my reflection, then leave the restroom.

The room is loud, buzzing with conversation and the soft orchestral music playing on a raised stage across the room. Locating a bar, I start in its direction, hoping to obtain just the smallest bit of liquid courage to get me started tonight.

"Annabelle Murphy?" a deep voice questions to my right.

I turn toward the voice, a wide smile lifting my cheeks. "Jack Thompson!"

We walk toward each other, and he bends, placing a kiss

on my cheek. "Annabelle Murphy." He glances down to my left hand. "It is still Murphy?"

I laugh. "Yes, still Murphy." I grasp onto his arm and give it a little shake. "It's been a long time, Jack! What are you doing in New York?"

He nods, smiling, dimples exaggerating his already handsome face. "Years, I think." He nods in the direction of the bar. "Were you headed that way? Would you like a drink?"

"I'd love one."

He takes my hand, placing it in the crook of his arm, and walks with me to the bar, looking down at me. "Is it possible that you've gotten more beautiful over time?"

"I was just wondering the same thing about you," I tease, thinking just how handsome he had, in fact, become with age. We grin at each other, turning our attention to the selection of cocktails at the bar.

"What would you like?" he asks, still holding my hand in his arm.

"Champagne, please."

He signals the bartender and orders two. When we have our glasses in hand, he suggests finding a table to sit at. We find one only partially occupied and sit.

"So, tell me, what brings you to New York?" Bringing the glass to my lips, I take a sip, the taste sweet as bubbles pop below my nose.

He lowers his glass after taking a sip. "I was actually in town to do a lecture at the University Hospital and was invited to stay for the event. I had no plans for the weekend, so I thought, what the hell." His cheeks dimple again as he meets my gaze. "And I think I'm glad I did."

"I'm going to assume you aren't married either then?" I lift a brow, hiding my curiosity behind my glass as I take another sip.

"Not anymore." One side of his mouth curls into a lopsided smile.

We spend the next fifteen minutes chatting, both of us finishing our drinks. He offers to go get us two more, which I gratefully accept. My eyes sweep across the expanse of the room, taking in all the sights, sounds, and colors. It's been several minutes, so I glance in the direction of the bar, looking for Jack. My breath catches in my throat when I lock eyes with the very last person I ever expected to be here. We stare at each other, my heart galloping against my breast bone, until a very tall, very beautiful woman steps between us and slides an arm around his waist.

Holy shit. I stand and grasp onto my clutch. I need to leave. There is absolutely no way I can be in the same vicinity as him. I'm about to turn when, suddenly, Jack is standing beside me. I must have a bewildered look on my face because one of concern appears on his features. "Are you okay, Annabelle?"

"Oh, yes." I force a smile in his direction. "I'm not feeling well all of a sudden. I think maybe the champagne isn't agreeing with me."

He moves to place our drinks on the table then takes me by the elbow. "Here, let me help you. Can I get you a cab? See you home?"

Jesus, why does he have to be so perfect? And what in the hell is god damn Patrick Connors doing here? "I'll be fine. I have a car waiting." I tip up on my toes and drop a quick kiss on his cheek. "Thank you for being such a gentleman. It was lovely catching up with you."

"Here." He reaches inside his coat pocket, extracting a business card. "Call me when you're feeling better." He gives me a small smile. "I'm only a short flight away. I'd love to see you again."

I take the card and nod. "That would be lovely." I squeeze his hand once then release it as I turn and walk away. I'm trying not to scurry like a mouse, but I feel like, at any moment, there will be a snap and I'll be trapped. I make it to the exit of the ballroom, breathing a sigh of relief as I sweep through the doors. I stop several feet down the hall to fish in my clutch for my phone and the driver's card.

"Running away?" My hand freezes, every hair on my body prickling at the sound of his voice. "I didn't even get to ask you for a dance." His footsteps come to a stop directly behind me. "You look radiant in this dress." His fingers brush across my shoulder then trail down my arm, wrapping around my elbow. He pulls, turning my body to face him.

"You look beautiful." His eyes are adoring as he releases my elbow, lifting his palm to my cheek, my voice apparently lost. He slides his hand through my hair to cup the back of my head and leans toward me.

I think he's going to kiss me, but instead, he inhales deeply, pressing his nose against the top of my head. My lids flutter shut as the heat of his breath blows against my forehead. After a moment, he looks down at me, my eyes meeting his. His face is only two inches from mine. "You didn't come."

My brow creases as I squint, confusion swirling through

me. I open my mouth to speak, close it, then open it again. "What?"

He grips the back of my head tighter, pulling me another inch closer, his voice low. "I'm not your client anymore. I thought you would come to see me."

My eyes dart to his lips then back up to his irises, green and bright. "I just—" My mouth feels so dry. I swallow. "I didn't think it was a good idea."

He scoffs, letting go of me as he takes a step back, crossing his arms. *Jesus, he looks good in a tux.* "Why did you quit as my therapist then?"

I shake my head, stuttering. "I-I didn't think we were a good fit."

He uncrosses his arms, stepping into my space again. "Liar. You're attracted to me. As much as I am to you. That's why you came to the club looking for me that night. That's why you quit as my therapist. And it's why I practically made you come on your desk when I kissed you."

He's right. Every single thing he's saying is true. I do want him. I want him to throw me over his knee again. Spank me. Thrust his fingers into me. I want him to drive his cock into me as I scream out his name. But I've never been the aggressor. Ever. I have no idea how to deal with a man like him. I glance up, not brave enough to utter even one of these things.

Hissing in frustration, he grips my forearms. "Why won't you say anything?"

"I want you," I confess on a whisper, peeking up under my lashes. My cheeks flush from the heat flaring beneath my skin.

"Then leave with me." His hold on me softens.

"Now?" My pulse quickens at the thought. He isn't my patient anymore. Then I remember the woman who wrapped her arm around him at the bar. "Aren't you here with someone?"

"Shit." He stomps backward and rakes a hand through his hair. "Yes, but it's not what you think. She's a friend."

"A very attractive friend," I mumble.

He pushes me, forcing my back against the wall, and slams his mouth over my lips, his hands locking around my face. I gasp, giving his tongue all the permission it needs to sweep inside and duel with mine as he presses his body flush to mine. The kiss is almost brutal in its intensity, passion overriding any doubts I just had. As suddenly as the kiss began, it stops with him tearing away from me, growling. "She's a friend. And she has absolutely nothing on you."

"Okay."

"Trick?" It's a woman's tentative voice.

"Fuck." He drops his hands from my face and spins around, blocking the woman from view, and addresses her. "Charlie, I'm sorry."

"Is everything okay?"

I wipe my fingers around my lips, hoping my lipstick isn't smeared over half my face, and step out from behind my hiding spot. I'm startled when I realize this isn't the same woman he was with at the bar, even more so by the fact that she's quite pregnant. "Excuse me, I'll let you two talk."

I start to step away, but a strong grip clutches my wrist. "Don't go. This will only take a minute."

"Really, it's fine." I yank my wrist from his grasp. "I was leaving anyway."

"I'm sorry." The other woman walks up to me. "I didn't mean to interrupt." She gives me a warm smile. "I just wanted to let Trick know I'm tired and that Gabby will drop me off if he wants to stay."

"Do you want me to take you?" He steps closer to her, concern drawing his brows low.

"Don't be silly." She motions toward the ballroom. "Gabby was looking for any excuse to leave so she can go abuse her cop." Her eyes dart from him to me and then back to him. "It looks like you're in the middle of something anyway."

"I don't need Trey trying to rip my dick off later if you don't get home safely," he grumbles.

"I have a New York City police officer escorting me home, Trick. What could be safer?" She laughs. "I'm fine. Go." She shoos him away from her then looks over at me as she walks away. "Take good care of him."

He's in front of me before I can blink, his hand reaching for mine. "Let's go."

"I have a driver," I state.

"Call him."

He waits as I pull out my phone and the card for the driver. I dial the number, my fingers shaking, and tell him I'm ready. "He'll be out front in five minutes."

"Okay. Do you have a jacket? A wrap?"

I nod. "At the coat check. Near the entrance."

"Come." He slides an arm around my waist and guides me in that direction. When we reach the counter, I hand the attendant my ticket. She returns in seconds, exchanging my wrap for a ten that Patrick hands her. He swings the wrap around my shoulders, pulling it closed at my neck, his eyes locking onto mine. "That's the last time tonight I plan on putting something on you instead of taking it off."

I lick my lips, nodding as he puts his arm around me and guides me outside to the waiting car, where I wonder if I'm making the best or the worst decision of my life.

CHAPTER TWELVE

~Trick~

The ride is fucking torture. I've been trapped in the back of this car for almost twenty minutes, her delicate hand in mine. I trace my thumb back and forth against her smooth skin, my restraint close to snapping. Although neither of us has spoken a single word, so much is being said in that one touch. I want her entire body in my arms, every inch of her flesh against my own, her mouth on mine.

She gave the driver her address when we got in the car, and that's fine with me. Whatever makes her comfortable. Besides, now I'll know where to find her after this. She squeezes my hand. "We're almost there."

"Okay," I practically snarl, the beast in me ready to attack. The car comes to a stop two minutes later, and I step out, pulling her behind me before the driver can even open his door. I hand him a twenty through the window. "Thanks."

We're standing between two buildings, leaving me unsure which way to turn. "Which one is yours?"

She tugs my hand to the right, leading me to the correct entrance. "This way." I follow her into the lobby and then the elevator. She presses the number nine then steps back beside me. I peer down at her, desire so strong I'm sure my eyes are dark with lust. My cock twitches when her tongue peeks out between her lips to trace them slowly. She's teasing me.

"Don't," I rumble, stepping closer to her, backing her against the wall.

Her head tilts back, eyes wide, her chest rising quickly. "Don't what?"

"Don't push me." I place my hands on the wall beside her head, leaning down. "I'll throw you up against this wall and fuck you right here. And I won't stop until I come."

Her teeth sink into her lower lip as she nods in understanding. I'm a fraction of an inch away from sliding my mouth over hers when the elevator pings to a stop, the doors parting. She blinks, looking over my shoulder. "Saved by the bell."

I scoff. "Only for a minute." Her hand claims mine as we step out into the hallway then turn to the right. She stops in front of a door labeled 9D, pulling a set of keys out of the little black bag she's carrying. Her hands are shaking as she tries to insert the key, so I take it from her, stick it into the lock, and turn. I push through the door, holding it open for her, then walk through and close it.

After tossing the keys on a table next to the door, I stride straight to her, my hand finding the back of her neck as I crash my mouth against hers. The bag she was holding hits the floor, and a second later, her hands are clutching at the lapels of my jacket as we slam our bodies together. She kisses me hard, her need as hungry as mine. Her tongue presses against my lips, forcing them open as she plunges inside, stroking it greedily against mine.

I pull back and nip her bottom lip then suck it gently into my mouth, sweeping my tongue over my teeth marks. She moans, twisting herself out of my grasp, stepping back, her eyes wild as she pants out quick little breaths.

"Wait." She holds a hand up, face flushed pink, when I move to draw her back to me.

"What's wrong?" I stop, reaching my hand up to her face, wondering if I bit her too hard.

"Will you dance with me?" she rushes out.

"What?" I'm momentarily confused by the shift in gears. "You want me to dance with you?" *I'll dance with you, between the sheets, slamming in and out you. I'll make you twist and shout and do the shimmy-shake if you'll just fucking let me.*

She nods, her eyes meeting mine. "I know it's dumb." Then she sweeps a hand over her skirt. "It's just that I put on this fancy dress and these fancy shoes." She kicks a pointed toe out from under the material. "And now I have the perfect partner. I just want one dance."

My face softens realizing that, no matter how tough she may be on the exterior, inside she's just a woman. A woman who wants to dance with a man. And I can do that for her. As easily as I breathe. "There's no music." I step closer to her, extending my arms in invitation.

She walks into my waiting arms, one hand slipping into

mine, the other falling onto my shoulder. "Alexa, play something from my sexy song Playlist."

I throw my head back and laugh. "You have a *sexy song* playlist?" I grin widely, teasing her.

"Doesn't everyone?" She shrugs and giggles. Soft music starts playing from the speaker, so I gather her closer, moving slowly in a circle to the rhythm. After a few seconds, I recognize the soulful voice of Sade, singing, "No Ordinary Love." As we turn, our bodies fuse closer together, heat blazing between us. Her hand slides off my shoulder and under my jacket, skimming up before resting flat on my pec.

My lips brush her temple, her cheek, her mouth, and then her neck as her head falls back. I pepper kisses across her shoulder, down her chest until I reach the edge of the velvet covering her breast. She stands straight, stopping our movement, and locks her stare with mine. She slips her hands under my jacket at each shoulder, pushing it off my body until it's laying on the floor.

She takes a step closer, her fingers reaching out to the buttons on my shirt, her lip clenched between her teeth as she undoes each one. When she gets to my waist, she yanks the excess material from my slacks, releasing the last two buttons. Her fingers graze up the open seam of my shirt before finally stroking inside to spread it wide, my chest now exposed. She places her hands flat on my stomach then looks up at me, her eyes wide.

"You're so beautiful," she whispers.

I feel my brows lift in surprise. Beautiful is the very last word I would use to describe myself. She shakes her head to stop any denial she must sense I'm ready to voice. "Don't."

She splays her hands wider and smooths them over my abs, moving them up until she's over my chest, one hand stopping over my piercing. "Does this hurt?"

She's staring at it, unaware I think, that she just licked her lips. I lift my hand to the thick metal hoop stuck through my nipple, pull it from between her fingers, and give it a small tug. "No." I meet her dark stare. "It feels good."

She breaks her gaze to lean forward and, surprising me, latches her mouth around the nipple, catching the ring in her teeth, and sucks. My hips surge forward, my cock instantly hardening, a hiss escaping my mouth. "Fuck, Belle." My hand clutches onto the back of her head, my fingers threading through her hair as I grip tightly. She sucks harder, her hands gripping onto my chest, her nails biting into my skin.

I moan, releasing my hold on her to rip the shirt completely off my body, one hand reaching down to squeeze my shaft as she continues sucking. Just when I think I'm going to have to yank her off me, she slides her mouth off my swollen bud and glides her tongue down to the middle of my abs, falling to her knees in front of me. She peeks up at me as she begins working the belt on my trousers, her fingers making quick work of the button next.

"Belle—" I state hesitantly, knowing what she's about to do, not sure if I can last more than two minutes if she puts me in her mouth.

"Shh," she coos up at me as my pants drop down to my knees. "I want to taste you." My cock springs up, a small gasp falling from her O shaped mouth as she looks down. My cock isn't some giant thing girls are going to run screaming from. It's an average length, but it's thick—thicker than most

—probably making it seem larger than others and maybe more daunting. Her eyes dart up to mine, but it's not fear I see. It's desire. Her tongue sweeps across her lips, the corners raised slightly.

"If you keep looking at me like that, I'm going to come before you even put me in your mouth," I growl out.

"Don't come in my mouth, okay?" she says, and before I can answer, she leans forward and drags her tongue up the side of my dick like it's an ice cream cone, pushing it inside her mouth when she reaches the top. Wet heat surrounds my cock. My head falls back as she slides her mouth lower, a groan rolling up from my chest in pure fucking pleasure.

When she seems to have gone as far down as she can go, she swallows, gagging, the muscles in her throat squeezing around my cock. I reach out and grab her head, forcing her to stay there a minute. Her mouth feels so fucking good wrapped around my dick. She gags again, her hands digging into my thighs as I thrust once before pulling her back. She pants, drool dripping from her lips, as she peers up at me. Red, billowy material surrounds her like a cloud, and I swear, I've never seen anything sexier. She keeps her gaze locked on mine as she sucks my cock back between her glossy lips, not resisting when I tighten my grip. I shove myself deep, causing her to gag again, her eyes watering as she chokes on my dick. I pull back, and she sucks hard as I do, my balls tightening, her head bobbing up and down on my cock.

"Stop. I'm gonna—." I clench my fingers in her hair and pull her off of me, moaning loudly as I come, my release exploding onto her bare chest and neck. She squeezes her hand around my shaft, rubbing back and forth until I'm done, my cock twitching as it begins to soften. My legs are shaking. I need to sit before I fall down, but I don't know if I ever want to leave this spot. She's looking up at me, her cheeks pink, swollen lips turned up in a shy smile, hair falling down her back. She's god damn perfection. Instead, I bend down, cup her cheek, and plant a kiss on her mouth. "That was amazing."

She kisses me back, running a hand through my hair. "Yes, it was." She sits back on her legs. "Could you get me a towel out of the bathroom." She looks down at her chest then points to a hallway. "It's down there. Second door."

"Of course." I stand and come back a minute later with a gray hand towel, freezing in place when I see the look on her face. "What's the matter?"

She rises slowly, her gaze wide as she reaches out to take the towel out of my hand. She wipes her chest clean, still looking at me, eyes crinkled as her brow furrows, her lips in a straight line.

"Jesus, Belle, tell me what's wrong? Did I hurt you?" I step closer, grabbing the towel out of her hand, throwing it on the counter.

"Your back." She shakes her head, her hand pointing over my shoulder. "Who did that to you, Patrick?"

Shit. I forgot about the fresh cane marks on my back. But she knows I like pain. We talked about this in our sessions, and she came to the club. She saw what was there, what could happen. "You already know this about me." I reach down and grab my shirt off the floor, moving to put it on, but she grabs it out of my hand.

"Don't try to hide it from me!" She stomps behind me,

gasping as she takes a closer look, her fingers grazing over some of the marks. "Why would you let someone hurt you like this?" Disbelief sounds in her voice.

"I told you before, I like it." I spin around, facing her, crossing my arms.

"Would you want me to do that to you?" she asks quietly.

"Would you want to?" I already know the answer, but like the asshole I am, I ask the question anyway.

"God, no!" She shakes her head furiously. "I couldn't. I couldn't hurt you like that."

I take a step closer. "Like how I hurt you when I spanked you?" I challenge.

"That's different," she tries to defend.

"How is it different?"

"It just is. You spanked me. Yes, it hurt, but you didn't beat me." She motions toward my back again. "That's abuse. Or torture, or something like it."

"It's not abuse if I ask for it. Crave it. Need it." I take another step closer and pull her to me, a gasp coming from her. "Don't tell me you didn't like it when I spanked you. That you didn't like the pain, the way it crept over your skin and down your spine, leaving every nerve feeling alive and tingling. How it made you so wet my fingers slid right inside you, your pussy sucking them in." I glare down into her eyes. "Can you deny it?"

Her nostrils flare as she stares back at me, finally answering. "No." She shakes her head. "But I'd never want to be beaten like you."

"Don't knock it 'til you try it." I shrug and release her.

She gapes up at me, taking a step back. "I think this was a mistake."

I grab my shirt from her hand and move to put it on, sighing. "This wasn't a mistake." I begin fastening the buttons. "You're afraid."

"Afraid?" She scoffs. "Afraid of what? Being beaten?"

I roll my eyes. "You're afraid of what you're feeling. Afraid of how good it felt when I spanked you. Afraid because you want me to do it again." I lean down to pick my jacket up off the floor, hovering my face over hers when I rise. "Afraid that you might even enjoy something more." I lower my voice. "But mostly, I think you're afraid because you want all those things from me. And what kind of a person would want to be with a monster like me?"

Her mouth falls open, but she remains silent.

"And now you can't say anything because you're afraid I'm right." I shrug my jacket on and stride over to her, grasping her face in my hands. "I want you more than anything I can ever remember wanting, and being here with you tonight was incredible, but I won't force you to be with me. I won't force you to do something with me that you're not ready for." I kiss her then, her mouth barely registering the action, then I release my hold and walk to the door. "You know where to find me."

CHAPTER THIRTEEN

~Annabelle~

The clock's second hand ticks a full circle, the large hand clicking onto the five. It's five minutes after his normal appointment would have started. Of course, he's not here. I told him I couldn't work with him anymore. For some reason, though, I haven't filled his time in my calendar with any other clients. It's been almost a full week since he stood in my apartment, his back bruised and scarred, my fear gripping and commanding.

There was a part of me that thought he might still show up. Maybe not on Monday, but today. Our regular Friday appointment. I mean, it has been almost a week. But of all the things Patrick is, or was, he was never late. He was always punctual. His military discipline, I suppose.

I open his file and scan through some of my notes. He was never very forthcoming with anything he decided to tell me. I always had to drag or coerce information from him. It took three weeks before he told me that both of his parents died in a small plane crash when he was only ten. A plane that his father was piloting. His father had been taking his mother away to Martha's Vineyard for a weekend getaway. The plane ended up in the ocean. He didn't tell me anything else about their deaths. I'm not sure if he even knew.

His grandmother raised him, sending him to West Point in his father's footsteps, where he graduated at the top of his class. This I knew from his military records, not from any information he had shared. He was selected for the Army Air Assault School, and again, graduated one of the top candidates in his class. He became part of the 101st Airborne Division, which specializes in air assault operations, based in Fort Campbell, Kentucky.

In 2016, the brigade was deployed to Iraq to assist with Operation Inherent Resolve. In December 2017, two weeks before his tour was to end, his helicopter was shot down by an RPG missile, killing three of the four crew members on board. He was the lone survivor. He broke the lower tibia and fibula of his left leg, sustained a concussion, took six stiches above his right eye, and suffered burns on his hands. He was honorably discharged from the Army after spending three weeks in a German hospital base.

He had been referred to me by another colleague who had advised that Patrick suffered from nightmares, guilt, and other traumatic, stress related symptoms. He wanted to fly again, but because he was involved in a crash, the FAA required psychiatric evaluation and clearance. Unable to get Patrick to open up, he sent him to me. We see how well *that* worked out. My attraction to him resulted in actions I'm not proud of, and now I'm questioning my judgment as a professional at all.

The thing is, I really do want to help him. This is more than a job to me. It truly matters to me to be able to help someone. There are too many stories of soldiers returning from war that commit suicide. I know all too well what that does to a family.

I glance at the picture of my mom and I on the corner of my desk. I'd put most of the pictures of my dad away in a drawer. I had tried to forgive him, but some days, the anger over what he did was just too much. We deserved more. He deserved more. But back then, when my father served, there was a negative stigma attached to anyone who couldn't withstand the pressures of war. You were deemed weak or mentally incompetent if you needed help.

I pick up my phone and dial my mom.

She answers on the third ring. "Hey, sweetheart. This is a nice surprise." Just hearing my mom's voice lifts my mood.

"Hey, Momma. I have a break between clients and started thinking about you."

"Well, I was just sitting down to have a cup of coffee, so your timing couldn't be better."

"Momma?" We don't talk about what my father did very often, so I'm afraid to broach the subject with her. "Do you think we could have done anything to save Dad? Should we have done something more?"

"Oh, honey." My mom lets out a long sigh. "I don't know. Your father had a lot of demons haunting him when he came back from Afghanistan. Remember, he'd been stationed there for almost two years."

"Did you know how bad it really was?" I pause. "I guess what I'm asking is, did you think he would ever do what he did?"

"No." She sniffles, and my heart sinks, turning my stomach, knowing I'm causing her pain. "Never."

"I'm sorry, Momma. I didn't want to upset you."

"I know, I know." She sniffles again. "No matter how much pain your father was in, I just thought he loved us more, or enough that it would see him through it."

"What do you mean?" My brows furrow.

"I thought me loving him, and him loving us, would be enough to ease his pain. But it just wasn't. He needed something more. Something else. He had no way to deal with all of that pain, all the memories. I just wish I had known a way to help him. Because, Belle, I don't care what it would have taken to ease that for him, as long as it meant he might still be here today."

Her words sink deep, their meaning so much more than she can realize. Patrick and his guilt. His need for pain. The punishment his release.

"I wish he was still here, too. But, Momma?"

"Yes?"

"I'm so glad I still have you."

"Oh, honey, me too. I love you."

"I love you, too. I'll talk to you soon, okay?"

"Okay, bye, honey."

"Bye, Mom."

I hang up the phone. I know now, without a shadow of a

doubt, that Patrick would never hurt me. He wouldn't want or expect that from me either. His pain is for a very different reason, one that I know I can help him with. But I wonder how far he'll go to continue to ease his pain and his guilt.

~

Sitting through the rest of the day with my clients has never been harder, because all I want to do is go and see Patrick. But I had already cancelled all my client appointments the Friday before, so I am not doing that again. I have been more than unprofessional in my actions with one client; I refuse to do it to anymore.

Finally, after my last appointment, I get in a cab and head to his apartment. I didn't call. I have his number on file, so I could have. He left me last week stating I know where to find him, so I'm throwing caution to the wind and just going. My appointments end at four on Fridays, so it's early enough in the day that I'm hoping I can catch him at home.

The cab pulls up to the curb in front of the address I provided, and I hand the driver the fare before stepping out onto the sidewalk. I take a deep breath, turn, and stop mid-stride. Patrick's jogging down the street, wearing a pair of shorts, his shirt tucked into his waistband, and his puppy panting in his arms. I shake my head, not quite sure what I'm seeing is real, but it is. It's the end of March, and while today is a relatively mild day in New York City at around fifty-five degrees, it's still cold out.

I can tell when he notices me because his step falters, and the expression on his face changes to one of surprise, his eyes a bit wide. He comes to a stop in front of me, his chest heaving as he pants.

"Nice jogging accessory." I point at the dog then reach under his chin to give it a scratch.

"Yeah, he made it one mile, and then I had to carry him the other four." He looks down at the dog, exasperation on his face.

"Patrick, he's a puppy. They can't run five miles. They can barely walk around without tripping over their own feet when they're this small." I take the puppy from his hands, snuggle it against my chest, and start talking to it in a baby voice. "Kane, he doesn't know a thing about taking care of you, does he?"

I look up at him to find him staring down at me, his expression blank. He runs a hand through his sweaty hair, grimacing. "I need to take a shower. Do you want to come up?" He nods to his building.

"I wanted to talk to you," I state, not really answering.

"Then come up." He runs a hand down his chest, wiping the sweat away. Of course, my eyes fix on that damn nipple and the metal hoop stuck through it. And, of course, he notices, looking down to where my line of sight is fixed, and chuckles. "You can wash my back, or my front, if you want."

My eyes fly up to his, my mouth falling open to protest, but I don't. Because, oh my, the thought of soaping him up in the shower just caused a rush of heat to surge between my legs. He chuckles again, at my reaction I'm sure, and places a hand on my shoulder, guiding me toward the door. "Come on."

We climb in the elevator, and he leans over me to press

the number eight, his bare shoulder brushing against my arm sending a tingling sensation across my skin. My eyes scan the tattoo across his back. 'All Pain is Fleeting'. I find myself hoping that the statement is true as he straightens and looks over at me.

"Aren't you cold?" *In other words, please put your damn shirt on before I climb you like a tree and forget every other reason I came here.*

"Nope." He grins wickedly, taking pleasure in my discomfort. "Are you?"

"Me?" I ask stupidly.

He aims his gaze at my chest, and I glance down, horrified when I notice my nipples are pointed beneath my blouse. I feel my face flame in embarrassment as I try to shift the puppy to cover up my traitorous girls and glare back at him. "It's cold out."

"Uh-huh," he drawls, a knowing smile smirking his lips. The elevator comes to a stop, doors opening, and I step out in relief. One more minute in that confined space, with his scent invading my senses as much as his half-naked body, and I may have started dripping down my damn leg. I should have gone home and put on jeans instead of coming straight from work in this skirt.

He strolls ahead of me, opening the door to his apartment, then holds it for me and Kane as I pass through.

"You don't lock your door?" My brows arch up.

"Where would I have put the key?" He looks down at his body, of course bringing my attention to it again, and I roll my eyes. "Besides, I have a dog now. He'll protect me."

I look down at the puppy, sleeping like a log in my arms, and give him a lopsided smile. “Yeah, okay.”

He walks further into the apartment, pulling the t-shirt out of his waistband and tossing it onto the back of one of the stools as he walks into the kitchen. He opens the fridge, grabs a water bottle, and proceeds to chug its contents in five seconds flat. He throws the empty bottle away then looks up at me. “You want something to drink?”

I shake my head. “No.”

“I’ll be ten minutes.” He points to the bathroom. “Unless you want to join me.” He looks over at me, one brow arched seductively.

I nod, staring dumbly at him. “No, I’ll wait here.”

He chuckles. “You sure?” He starts toward the bathroom, a smug smile on his face. “I’ll keep the door unlocked, just in case.”

He winks as he shuts the door behind him, and I look up at the ceiling, mumbling out loud. “Jesus, Joseph, and Mary. I’ve never wanted to take a damn shower so bad in my whole life.”

I walk around the apartment to see if I can find a bed to put the dog in, but don’t see one. It’s possible it’s in the bedroom, but there is no way I am stepping foot in there. I place him on the couch, smiling when he lets out a little whimper then rearranges himself into a tight ball and falls back asleep.

I take my purse that had been hanging over my shoulder and put it on the floor next to the couch. I shrug the open cardigan I’m wearing off, placing it on top of my bag, then walk around looking at things.

There's not a lot to look at. His coffee table is scattered with game cartridges, remotes, and a couple empty beer bottles. He has a huge flat-screen mounted to the wall, above a cabinet that holds various electronic equipment. There's a bunch of built in bookcases on one wall, so I walk over to check out what he has. Lots and lots of Stephen King, and then text books. Lots of military based and historical books.

There are two pictures in the corner on one of the shelves. One is of the pregnant girl I saw at the Ball. She's hugging a man, who I'm going to assume is her significant other. The other is of a couple in their later thirties or early forties. I pick it up and study it. From the style of clothing they're wearing, I'm going to guess it was taken in the nineties, and I wonder if they're his parents. The man in the picture bears a striking resemblance to Patrick.

The door to the bathroom swings open just as I'm setting the picture back down. Patrick emerges from a cloud of thick, heavy steam, a dark blue towel wrapped around his waist, water dripping from the ends of his hair onto his chest. I blink and then turn away from him, knowing my body, if not my expression, will give away the arousal he's stirring up in me.

I jump when I feel his fingers wrap around mine, pulling me back around. "Come with me." It's a demand, not a request, his voice husky. My feet respond, following when he leads me into his bedroom, what I want to talk to him about momentarily forgotten.

CHAPTER FOURTEEN

~Trick~

I lead her into my bedroom, not bothering to turn the lights on, stopping when we reach the foot of my bed. I turn to face her, releasing her hand to place mine under her chin instead, lifting it until her eyes lock with mine. I brush my fingers against her cheek then skim lower, raising my other hand as I find the first button on her shirt and begin to work it.

"I've been waiting a week for you to come." I release the button and move to the next one. "I've taken Kane for six walks a day to kill time." Slide down to the next button. "I smashed my cell phone against the wall on Wednesday so I wouldn't call you." I graze my fingers even lower to the next button, my eyes still locked on hers. "I've drank myself into a stupor every night so I wouldn't go to your place." I feel down the seam of her shirt, finding the last button. "And I didn't go to the club. Not once. Because all I want is you."

Her shirt falls open, and I slide my hands around her waist, skimming my hands up over the bare flesh of her back and around to her smooth stomach. I trail my hands softly up and over her breasts, which rise and fall quickly under my touch, and finally over her shoulders, pushing her shirt off.

"Patrick," she whispers. "I have things I want to say to you."

I shake my head slowly back and forth. "Later." I lean forward, sliding my hand up to fist the back of her head as I tilt it up to me, my eyes blazing down at her. "I'm done waiting for you." I arch her head back farther and crush my mouth to hers, not pausing for her consent. The facts that she came, that she waited while I showered, and that she followed me into this bedroom gave me all the permission I need.

Her hands clasp onto my arms, her body melting into mine, and a moan sounds from her throat as I wrench her closer. I release the grip I have on her head to slide my hands down to her ass, jerking her against my throbbing cock. I find the zipper on the back of her skirt, pull it down, then let it slide down her legs. She steps out of the skirt and reaches over, ripping the towel off my waist at the same time.

Gripping under each thigh, I lift her onto the bed, her legs wrapping around me as I prowl over the top of her, my mouth fused to hers, our tongues devouring each other. I grind myself against her covered core, releasing her lips to nibble my way down her throat and over her lace covered breast.

She whimpers, her fingers weaving through my locks when I drag my tongue over one swollen nipple.

I release the clip on the front of her bra and remove it, letting her breasts spill free, and latch my mouth onto one puckered tip. I flick my tongue back and forth before I suck hard, sending her back bowing off the bed as she mewls out my name. My cock jerks against her thigh at the sound of my name tumbling from her lips. I release the hard peak with a soft pop and rise to crash my mouth back to hers, sweeping my tongue deep, my hunger for her flaring intensely with every groan.

She clenches her legs around my waist, thrusting her center against my stiff cock, dragging her wet panties up and down my length. I can feel her nails biting into the skin of my back as she clings onto me, and I find myself wishing she would rake them down my back. I want to feel the pain of my skin slicing open as she rubs against me, but I push the thought away, knowing this is something different. Something bigger. Something better if I let myself feel it.

I break our kiss to lift myself off her, kneeling and then moving to stand at the foot of my bed, her body splayed out before me. She's fucking gorgeous. The most beautiful thing I have ever seen. And she's here, for me.

She sits up on her elbows. "What's wrong?"

I shake my head. "Absolutely nothing." I reach down and pull her heels off, then grip the edges of the black lace on her hips and slide them down her legs, dropping them to the floor. I find her eyes and stare back at her. "You're fucking perfect."

She sucks her bottom lip between her teeth, her lids

lowering halfway as she watches me crawl back up between her legs. She spreads them wider as I move higher, her hand slipping over her lips, her fingers moving to spread them for me. I growl at how uninhibited she is, my cock aching to be buried inside her. I lower my head and swipe my tongue up her clit. The salty taste of her explodes against my tongue, and I hum in approval.

I glance up, my pulse thrumming in excitement as I watch her head fall back and her mouth form a small O when I slide a finger into her drenched core. I flick my tongue over her clit, back and forth, sliding another finger in, pumping in and out, my cock dripping with need. She wriggles underneath, pushing herself up into my face, the stubble of my chin grinding against her folds, while her cries tell me not to stop.

I do though, right as I feel her muscles begin to clench around my fingers. I pull them out, a gasp of outrage coming from her as I raise my body over hers. I line myself with her core and start pushing my cock into her entrance.

"Go slow," she pants, her eyes clenching tight.

I nod my head, sliding forward as slowly as I can, allowing her walls to expand around the width of my cock. She's so fucking tight. When I'm finally all the way in, I groan so loud in pure fucking ecstasy, I'm sure every neighbor on my floor probably hears it. Rearing back slowly, I push forward once, twice, then again, the heat of her pussy the sweetest hell I've ever felt. I moan again, then freeze, pulling myself completely out of her. "Fuck!"

She sits up, eyes wide, brows raised high. "What?"

I run a hand through my still damp hair and shake my head, disgusted at myself. "Condom." I point down to my very angry dick, red and swollen against my waist. "I forgot. I'm sorry."

She sits up further, her features relaxing. "I have an IUD." Her eyes dart to my dick, her voice softening. "Are you clean?" She licks her lips then looks back up at me. "I mean, I know you spend a lot of time at that club." She frowns. "And of course, let's not forget about your job at Temptations. I'm sure you've done more than *escort* your dates."

I look down at her, surprised. "I'm clean. Everyone has to be tested there, and I always wear something if I'm, you know, *escorting* someone. Which I'm not anymore, by the way. Not since I've met you."

"Then how about you finish what you started?" She raises one brow, crooks a finger at me, and lies back on the bed.

"With pleasure." I kneel back between her legs, lift her knees, and sink into her in one thrust.

"God, yes!" echoes across the room as I bury myself inside her. I slide back slowly then shove forward, plunging deep inside her. I release her knees and move my body over hers, claiming her lips again as I continue to rock into her. She pushes against me, sliding her body out from under mine in one quick motion, my dick slipping free.

"I want to be on top." She grabs my arm and rolls me onto my back, straddling me.

"Okay," I pant, planting my grip on her hips as she tilts

them, sliding down onto my cock, stopping when she's fully seated.

She lets out a long moan as she begins gliding herself back and forth, her clit rubbing against the base of my cock, her head back, her long hair dusting against the top of my legs. I shift, moving to a sitting position, and her legs wrap tightly around my waist. I lean forward, sucking one of her raised buds into my mouth.

"Oh!" she exclaims, her hips jerking at the added sensation. I bite, hard, and groan when I feel her pussy clenching my dick like a vise. *She likes the fucking pain as much as I do.*

I release the grip my other hand has on her waist, and raise it to fist her hair, yanking her head back, biting again on her nipple, a scream of pleasure coming from her. I shove my cock higher, harder, deeper. Her muscles contract then release, a continuous pulsing throb as she comes, her nails scratching across my shoulders as she calls out my name again and again. I follow a second later, shouting obscenities, my vision going temporarily black as my release bursts inside of her, filling her with my seed as she continues to rock against me, my arms crushing her to me.

Her hips gradually come to a stop, our panting breaths the only sound in the room, while her heartbeat thuds against my chest. Her arms hang loosely around my neck, her head in the crook of my neck, her breath warm as she speaks. "I didn't come here for this."

I scoff, knowing she did, even if she won't admit it. "Yes, you did." I rock my hips. "Could you at least wait until my cock's not buried in you to deny it?"

She pushes against me to get up, but I tighten my arms around her, holding her against me.

"Stop." I sigh. "Just stop."

"Stop what?" She huffs against my shoulder, surrendering her struggle.

"Stop fighting me. Fighting this." I pull back to look at her. "You want this as much as I do."

She stares at me, blinking several times, her body softening against mine as she shakes her head in defeat. "I don't know what I want."

"You do." I place my finger under her chin and lift her face to me. "You're just still afraid to admit it." I press my lips to hers in a soft kiss. "It's okay to want this beast."

She kisses me back timidly, a soft chuckle following as she shakes her head. "How apropos."

My brows furrow. "In what way?"

"It doesn't matter." She shifts again, lifting her hips, but I lock my grip around her waist, trapping her in place.

"Tell me," I demand.

"It's stupid." Her cheeks flame red.

"I'll decide that." I shove up into her pussy, just the feel of her making me hard again. "Tell me or I'll throw you over my knee and spank you."

Her eyes dilate, and I realize I just doled out the wrong warning if I want her to comply. I push my cock up again and drawl out, "And, I won't fuck you after I do it."

Her eyes flare, but she heeds the warning. "My full name is Annabelle, but everyone calls me Belle, mostly because it's what my mother always called me." She twists a piece of her hair around her finger as she continues speaking, peeking up at me under her long lashes. “Her favorite fairy tale was *Beauty and the Beast.*” She laughs in memory. “She must have read it to me hundreds of times, telling me that someday I would find my prince. But she warned that I had to always remember that, sometimes, the most wicked of men turned out to be the best of men, so I should never overlook the beast.”

“Am I supposed to be the monster in this little story?” I ask sardonically.

“You’re not a monster,” she whispers. “I’m sorry.” She grabs my face with both hands, peppering kisses against my lips. “I’m sorry.”

I wrap my hands around her face, deepening the kisses she’s giving me. Her arms slide around my neck, her breasts pushing against my chest as she fuses herself against me. I slide my hands to her legs to unwrap them from my waist and lower her back onto the bed, shifting myself over her. My cock slides out for a moment, my cum running out of her. The sight makes me even harder, and I grip my cock in my fist, stroking it once before I shove it back into her core.

She’s so wet, I glide right in, my size no longer an issue. I slip my arms under her shoulders, hauling her body against mine, increasing the pace of my thrusts. Her arms clench around my body, her teeth sinking into my shoulder when I plunge deeper, harder, faster. My hips piston against hers, and I feel the skin between her teeth rip, the flesh under her nails tear, my cock swelling harder in response. I slam into her again and again, my balls bunching up, until I fucking explode, a roar bellowing from my chest as I pump every last drop of myself into her.

CHAPTER FIFTEEN

~Annabelle~

Patrick's body collapses on top of mine, our bodies slick with sweat and cum, both of us breathing heavily. I weave my fingers through his hair, feeling heat pulsate up from his scalp, and plant a kiss on his shoulder. I lick my lips, wet after kissing him, and taste blood. My eyes fly to his shoulder, and I see blood oozing from several punctures that my bite left.

"Oh my God!" My hand flies up to cover my mouth, Patrick rising up on his knees in alarm.

"What?" His eyes are wide, scanning my body. "Did I hurt you?"

I shake my head, lowering my hand from my mouth to point to his shoulder. "I hurt *you*."

He glances down to his shoulder and then back at me, brows furrowed. "That?" He lifts his shoulder, glancing down at it again. "That's a fucking love bite." He lowers himself, rolling next to me, propping his head up on his elbow. "Meaning, I love that you bit me." He traces a finger over the bite mark, smearing some of the blood. "It felt fucking incredible."

I stare back at him, speechless. He likes the pain. He apparently likes a little blood, too. But who am I kidding? So do I. I came undone the minute he bit down on my nipple. How could I not know this about myself? How could I be thirty-one years old and not know what turns me on sexually?

"What are you thinking?" He swipes his fingers across my forehead, pushing a lock of hair behind my ear. "I can see your mind is going a million miles an hour."

"How did you know?" I ask, my voice barely above a whisper. "How did you know that I would like the pain?"

"I didn't." He leans over, placing a tender kiss against my lips. "Not until you came to the club that night, when you let me spank you." He moves his lips lower and wraps them around my nipple, sucking gently, swiping his tongue over the tip when it peaks. "The way you responded. You weren't scared. You were excited, and you were so wet."

He blows against my nipple and I moan. "Stop. You're turning me on again."

He peers up at me, a devilish grin on his face. "Then I'll have to fuck you again."

My pussy actually contracts at his warning, shocking me. I've never had sex more than once in a night. It was all I could do to get through one time with my past partners, pretending it was great, pretending I came. Finishing myself off in the bathroom when they were done so I wouldn't hurt their feelings. And now, I'm ready to let him do whatever he wants to me, again. After only ten minutes.

He interrupts my thoughts, continuing to speak. "I wanted to fuck you so bad that night, especially when I realized it was you."

This gets my attention. I roll onto my side so I can look at him. "How did you know it was me? *How?* I was in complete disguise, right down to my eyes."

He chuckles, rising suddenly, moving toward the end of the bed. I admire his ass as he walks away, my gaze trailing up his back, my heart stuttering when I see the scratches I've left behind. *He's turned me into some kind of animal.* He leans his knees against the end of the bed, slides a hand under my foot, and lifts it, turning it so my ankle is facing up. He swipes his thumb over my tattoo then shoots his gaze up to mine. "Do you know how many times I looked at this tattoo when we were in your office as you crossed and uncrossed your legs in front of me, teasing me?" He bends and places a kiss over the ink. "So, when I pulled your boot off, I knew, instantly, that it was you."

I shake my head. My tattoo. It didn't even occur to me to hide it. I watch as he traces a finger around it, flashing his eyes back up to mine. "What's it mean?"

I laugh, remembering I had to tell him just moments ago about *Beauty and the Beast*. "It's the rose from the story my mom used to read to me."

He looks down at the flower and then back up at me, his expression blank.

"Do you seriously mean to tell me that you've never seen *Beauty and the Beast*, or at least heard the fairy tale?"

He shakes his head, shrugging his shoulders. "What can I say? I'm a guy's guy. I don't watch girly shit."

I roll my eyes. "We're going to have to change that. It's a classic."

He lowers my foot and sits on the bed, his expression changing to one more serious. "Why did you come to the club that night?"

I sit up, shifting around until I've loosened enough covers on the bed to pull some around me. I grimace when I realize I've wrapped most of the wet spot against my back, and drop the blanket.

Patrick gets up and yanks open a drawer on his dresser, then turns, handing me a gray t-shirt. "Here."

I take it gratefully, sliding it over my body, the soft material providing a thin layer of comfort. He reaches into another drawer, pulls on a pair of shorts, then comes to sit back beside me. "So?"

I sigh. "The club?"

He nods. "Was it to spy on me?"

My lips curve as I frown. "No, of course not." I pluck at a loose thread on the bottom seam of the t-shirt. "I was just curious."

"About me?" he pushes.

"No." I shrug. "And yes." I look up at him. "I wanted to understand how causing yourself so much pain could bring any pleasure whatsoever. I couldn't wrap my head around it. It didn't make sense to me. I just saw you bleeding and couldn't imagine what was done to leave you like that, and that it actually made you feel better."

"And now?" He looks down at the bite mark I left on his shoulder then back at me. "Now what do you think?"

"I'm scared," I admit, my focus shifting back to that loose thread.

"Are you scared of me?" he asks, concern edging his voice.

I shake my head. "No." I meet his gaze. "I liked what you did to me. How it felt when you spanked me. How it felt when you bit my nipple a few minutes ago. I'm scared because I've never felt like this before and because I want more. And, Patrick, I've never wanted more."

"Does that have to be a bad thing?" He tilts his head, eyes crinkling as he squints at me.

"I know I could never hurt you, and I know, right now, that's what you think you need."

"How do you know you can't give me what I need?" He tosses a hand in the air. "Two weeks ago, you didn't even know you liked to be spanked."

"You're right." I nod in agreement. "But I realized something today, and it's the reason I came to see you."

He grins. "I thought we already established why you came to see me."

I feel my face flush with heat, and I smile back at him, not denying that what just happened was amazing. I'm about to speak when barking sounds from the other side of the door.

"Shit." Patrick stands and strides to the door, opening it to find Kane standing on the other side, a fresh puddle of piss next to him. "Sorry, buddy." He reaches down, swiping the puppy up, and carries him with him as he leaves the room.

I climb down from the bed, find my panties, and slide them on under the shirt. Thankfully, because Patrick is so much taller than me, the shirt falls almost to my knees, essentially acting as a dress. By the time I get to the doorway, Patrick's back with paper towels and Lysol, bending down on his knees to wipe up Kane's accident. One side of his mouth dips down as he sprays the floor clean. "It's like having a god damn baby. Constantly feeding him, taking him to the bathroom, listening to him whine all fucking night. I'm going to get even with Charlie for this."

I notice Kane sits one foot away from Patrick, head between his paws, ears back, and so adorably guilty that I have to laugh. "How can you be mad at that?" I point to the puppy.

He turns to look at him, his features softening. "I'm not mad at him. I'm mad at Charlie. She's the one who dumped him on me."

I step over the mess and stoop in front of Kane, scooping him up in my arms. "He'll get better." I kiss him on his furry head and talk down at him. "Right, Kane?"

Patrick stands, a lopsided grin on his face as he rolls his eyes at me. "I have to feed him." The words are no sooner out of his mouth, when a loud grumble sounds from my stomach, Kane and Patrick both swinging their gazes to me. "And, I guess I need to feed you, too." He laughs.

He feeds the puppy while I use the bathroom to clean myself up. I honestly need a shower but do the best I can with a wash cloth I find in the cabinet and his man-scented body wash. He trades places with me, entering the bathroom when I'm done, and I keep an eye on Kane as he finishes his dinner. I walk over to the bar and find more than a dozen take-out menus lying there. I smile at his thoughtfulness and thumb through my choices.

He emerges a few minutes later, looking fresher and smelling delicious when he leans over me at the bar to place a kiss on my head. "Decide on anything?"

"I'd really love a pizza with the works." I look over my shoulder to find him beaming down at me in approval. "And wine. I could really use a glass of wine."

"A girl after my own heart, and wine I can do." He walks over to the fridge and pulls it open. "But, for now, do you want a beer? Or water?"

"Water, please."

He hands me a water and grabs a beer for himself, twisting the cap off before taking a hearty slug. "Can you call the pizza order in?" He points to the number on the menu. "Just tell them it's for Trick. They'll know where to deliver it."

I nod, taking a sip of my water, and answer. "Uh-huh."

"Cool, 'cause I kinda broke my phone." He grins widely. "I need to take this little guy outside for a minute, and I'll grab your wine, too. Red or White?"

"White. Anything but chardonnay."

He strolls into the bedroom, coming out wearing a fitted white t-shirt over a pair of sweats and sneakers. He attaches a leash to Kane, then scoops him up. "I'll be back in just a few minutes. Make yourself at home."

I find my purse over by the couch and sift through it until I find my phone. I place the order for the pizza then move to the couch and plop down. I fish through the remotes, trying a few to turn on the television, but it's hopeless. I toss my last attempt back on the table, and mutter out loud. "Where's Alexa when you need her?"

I almost piss my pants when an electronic voice speaks back. "I'm here. What can I help you with?"

I laugh out loud. "Alexa, turn on the T.V." I command.

"With pleasure." The television comes to life, the history channel logo displayed in the lower righthand corner. "Would you like me to change the channel?"

"Alexa, please turn the channel to CMT." I have no idea if Patrick has the channel, or if he likes country music, but the videos are always great if they're playing. I wait a second and smile when Keith Urban's face pops on the screen, his voice crooning how blue looks good on the sky.

A second later, the door swings open, and I grin, happy he's back so soon. I bounce up from the couch, turning, my gaze locking onto one as surprised as mine. It's the woman Patrick had his arm around standing in line at the ball. The same gorgeous woman, with long black hair, dressed in a sexy black dress and strappy heels, holding a bottle of tequila in one hand, her other on her jutted hip, smirking at me. "Well, what do we have here?"

CHAPTER SIXTEEN

~Trick~

I wait for what feels like fucking forever for Kane take a shit, then walk a block with him tucked under my arm to the nearest wine outlet. I grab two bottles of Pinot Grigio, every single person in the shop stopping me to fawn over the puppy before I can finally pay. I practically jog back to the apartment then pace back and forth in front of the elevator as I wait for it.

I'm worried she's going to start thinking again and bolt if I take too long. The lift arrives and delivers me to my floor, my senses going on high alert when I hear Gabby's voice drifting from my apartment. I pick up my pace, bursting through the open door into the apartment, absorbing the scene in front of me, my eyes locking onto Belle's angry face.

"Oh, look, here he is now," Gabby states in an overly dramatic voice. "Lover boy is back."

I swing my head in her direction, trying to figure out what the hell has happened. I slam the door behind me, setting the puppy on the floor and the wine on the counter. "What the fuck are you doing here, Gabby?"

"Charlie told me you'd been down in the dumps lately, so I thought I'd come cheer you up." She holds up a bottle of tequila then points her head in the direction of Belle, one brow arching high. "But looks like someone already beat me to it."

Belle's hands plant on her hips as she glares at me. "I thought you said you were just friends?"

"We are just friends. She has a damn boyfriend," I exclaim, turning to look at Gabby. "Tell her."

"I tried." She shrugs. "She didn't believe me. I told her just 'cause we fucked once upon a time doesn't mean we aren't friends now."

Belle visibly flinches like she's been slapped, and I snap. I see red as I storm up to Gabby and grab her by the arm. It's then that I smell her and realize she's drunk. "What the fuck is wrong with you? Why are you drunk at six o'clock?"

She wrenches her arm out of my grasp, almost losing her balance when she does, but grabs my shoulder before she can fall. "Don't touch me." She spins on her heel and heads for the door. "I'm leaving."

I step in front of her and block her exit. "Where the hell do you think you're going like this?"

She pushes against my chest, not even budging me. "I'm a big girl, Trick. Don't worry about me." She tries to walk around me, but I grab her wrist and pin her up against the door. I turn my head to Belle. "Can you call someone for me?"

"Let me go!" Gabby fights under me, slashing her nails down my arm.

I turn and hiss at her. "That won't work on me, remember?" I turn back to Belle, her eyes wide and fixed on me. "Can you dial 212-763-8558? Tell Charlie to come up to my apartment."

I watch as she dials the number, listening as she speaks. She hangs up. "She'll be right here." She gives me a blank stare then turns and walks across the room and into my bedroom, shutting the door behind her.

Gabby stops struggling against me, so I loosen my hold but don't release her. I know her well enough to know she'll bolt if she gets the chance. I bring my face to hers, and through gritted teeth, speak. "What the hell is going on with you?"

She smiles wickedly back. "Sorry I ruined your date. Looks like you got to fuck her already though, so not all's lost. Does she know how much you like—"

I've had enough. I step back, pulling her with me, yanking the door open at the same time, and push her out just as Charlie exits the elevator. "Take her before I do something I regret."

Charlie shoots me a confused look as she wraps an arm around Gabby.

I wave my arm in frustration. "She's drunk. Something's wrong, but instead of telling me, she went into full on bitch mode."

"Okay, I got her." She turns and leads Gabby to the elevator, the doors opening, and the pizza delivery guy steps out.

Jesus fucking Christ, what next? I pull a twenty out of my pocket and trade it with him for the pizza. When I go back inside the apartment, I stop in my tracks when Belle walks out of the bedroom, fully dressed. *I'm going to fucking kill Gabby.*

I toss the pizza on the coffee table on my way to her. "No, don't go." I reach her and latch onto her arms. "Please." I pull her closer to me. "I know that was the most fucked up ten minutes ever, but don't let it ruin our night." Her eyes blink up at mine, her head shaking back and forth. "I swear to God, she's a friend. She's Charlie's best friend, and, obviously, something's going on with her."

"You slept with her," she finally says.

I sigh, closing my eyes for a moment. "Yes. A few times. Over six months ago. It was sex. Nothing more. And not since."

"How many other fuck buddies can I expect to come knocking on your door?"

I raise my brows at the bite in her retort. She's feistier than I would have suspected. "None." I press my forehead against hers, forcing her to look at me. "I promise." I slide a hand into her hair and brush a kiss against her lips. "Stay."

After what feels like an eternity, she nods, and a wave of relief sweeps over me. I kiss her again. "I'm sorry," I murmur against her lips then fold her into my arms, grateful she's still here for me to hold.

"I could really use that glass of wine," she mumbles against my chest.

I chuckle, releasing her, dropping a kiss on her forehead. "Okay." I head to the kitchen. "Let me get some plates for the pizza, too."

She follows behind. "Can I help?"

I cock a brow. "You could go put my shirt back on so I know you're not going to leave."

She kicks her heels off, standing three inches shorter, so petite next to me, and smiles. "Will that do?"

"For now." I smile back at her, pulling the wine out of the bag. I place one bottle in the fridge and leave the other on the counter to open. I point toward the cupboards. "Plates are there, and glasses are up there if you want to grab one."

"Are you going to have a glass?" She walks over to where I directed.

"I'll stick with beer." I open the wine and pour a healthy portion into the glass she sets in front of me. She grabs a couple plates and her glass while I snatch up some napkins, forks, and a fresh beer, then she follows me back into the living room.

I sit and notice what's on. "Country?" I try not to make a face.

She sits beside me. "Not a fan?"

"I'm more of a rock 'n roll kind of guy." I shrug.

She laughs, sipping her wine. "And that doesn't surprise me one bit, Patrick."

I lean over and brush my lips across hers, the taste of the wine sweet when I swipe my tongue against hers, a warmth spreading across my stomach. "I like when you say my name," I muse softly. "Everyone always calls me Trick."

"Why does everyone call you Trick?" She reaches out to open the pizza box, putting a slice on each plate for us.

"It's a pilot thing." I take a bite of pizza, chew, then continue. "We all have call names, like a nick-name." I let out a snicker as I remember how I got my name. "I was a pretty damn good pilot but got into quite a bit of trouble. I tended to favor trickier maneuvers that were considered dangerous. And, thus, Trick was born."

"You mean, you *are* a good pilot."

I stop chewing and stare at her. "Not anymore." I grab the beer off the table and chug half of it, slamming it back on the table roughly, my pulse picking up when I look back at her. "You aren't going to ruin this and psychoanalyze me now, are you, Doc?"

"I think it's called getting to know each other," she answers, pressing her lips firmly together as she blinks over at me.

I close my eyes, letting out a sigh. "I'm sorry." I grab the bottle and take another swig. "I didn't mean to snap at you."

She nods and speaks softly, not giving up this subject easily. "I thought you wanted to fly again?"

I watch the video playing on the T.V. for a minute, then swing my gaze back to her. "I loved flying. I did." I take another drink. "I want to love it again. I just—" I look down at my feet and shake my head. "There's a history, ya know? Maybe this isn't what I'm supposed to do."

"You had more than one accident?" Her brows draw low as she drinks her wine.

I stand, needing another beer but also not wanting to see her reaction when I admit the next thought. "My father."

"Your father?" she replies, confusion in her voice. "How?" She pauses. I snag a beer out of the fridge and carry the wine bottle back with me. "You think because he crashed, too, that it's a sign? That you shouldn't fly?"

I refill her glass, place the bottle on the coffee table, and sink back into the couch, my elbows on my knees, my head hanging low between my shoulders. "Maybe."

"Patrick." She turns next to me, placing her palm against my cheek, and turns my face to hers. "I've read the reports. That crash wasn't your fault. Your helicopter was hit by a missile. There was nothing you could have done."

I press my lips into a frown, wanting to surge forward and kiss her, end this conversation, but I know it won't be that easy. So, I shrug. "I should have done more. I should have gotten my guys out of that chopper."

"Your leg was broken in two places. You had a concussion," she retorts, emotion in her voice, pleading my defense.

"I should have pushed through the pain. I should have gotten to them." I grimace. "At any cost. I'm a soldier first." I pull away from her and take a slug of my beer. "The pain would have faded."

"Your tattoo," she mumbles, thinking out loud. "All pain is fleeting."

I scoff. "Except, it's not." I stare back at her. "I'm in pain every fucking minute of every fucking day knowing that I lived and they didn't. They were burned alive, and I didn't do a damn thing to save them."

"Couldn't," she says. "You *couldn't* save them." She squeezes her hand on my thigh. "There's a difference, Patrick."

"Not to me," I mutter, shaking my head. "Not to me."

"So, you punish yourself." She slides her hand up to my face, pulling it back to hers again. "Let me help you."

I don't want to talk about this anymore, so I do what I know how to do best and surge forward, crushing my mouth against hers, wrapping my hands around her face. I hold her against me, forcing my tongue into her mouth, sweeping it against hers until I feel her surrender, her body giving in to me. Her arms snake around my neck, our kiss escalating in seconds.

Dragging her to her feet I begin undressing her, her fingers pushing down my sweats, our lips parting only long enough for me to yank my shirt over my head. We surge back together like two magnets connecting, my desire for her sparking a flame only she can tame. I fall back onto the couch, and she straddles my lap, her breaths panting out in quick bursts. She slides her core, wet and slippery, against the length of my cock and groans before slamming her mouth back to mine.

With one hand I grip her hip roughly to lift her, and use my other hand to guide my cock to her opening. I thrust my pelvis up as she surges down, both of us groaning. I clutch the back of her head and crash my mouth to hers again. I want to taste every moan that falls from her lips as I rock into her.

She shoves her head back, breaking the hold I have on her, sliding her hips back as she trails her tongue down my neck, over my pec, twirling the tip around my nipple before sucking my piercing between her lips. An electric shock bolts straight to my dick, my hips bucking hard, my cock throbbing against her tight muscles.

Sucking harder, she pumps her core back and forth on my cock frantically, over and over, until my release starts coiling up my balls, down my shaft, erupting as her walls convulse, sending me over the edge. She bites hard on my nipple, my fingers digging into the soft flesh of her ass, shoving my cock deep inside her as I yell out her name in relief.

CHAPTER SEVENTEEN

~Annabelle~

"Belle, will you go ask your dad to help with the groceries?" My mom set two bags on the kitchen table and begin unpacking one of them.

"Sure thing." I tug my coat off, dumping it unceremoniously on one of the chairs, which results in an eye roll from my mother.

"Really, Belle?" she chides.

"Fine." I huff, grabbing it off the chair, and hang it on a hook next to the door as I go in search of my dad. His office is in the basement, so I start there, assuming that's where he most likely is.

I open the door to the stairs, noting the lights are on and call out his name as I descend the stairs. "Dad?" I pause halfway down when he doesn't answer. My nose picks up a strange, coppery scent, wrinkling at the smell.

I tramp down the remainder of the steps, calling to him in a sing-song voice, "Daddy-O! We're home, and we have grocer—"

I turn the corner, noticing red and pink splatters on the wall first. My eyes dart lower to the pool of blood seeping in a large circle from behind my father's desk, white chunks floating in it. I run around the desk, my gaze locking onto the gun in my father's hand, sprawled beside his body, and I scream.

"Belle!" My eyes flutter open as I feel my body being shaken. I shoot to a sitting position, blinking rapidly, not recognizing my surroundings, my heart thundering against my chest.

"Belle?" I turn toward the cautious voice and remember I'm at Patrick's. I'm in his bed. I nod, my breathing erratic. "Are you okay? You were yelling for your mother."

I fling the covers off my body and slide out of the bed. When I glance down, I realize I'm naked and scan the dark room in search of the shirt I borrowed earlier from Patrick. I hear him rise from the bed, then feel the heat of his body as he wraps his arms around me and pulls me up against his chest.

I let out a strangled sob, wrapping my arms around him, clinging to him, tears cascading down my face. He squeezes me tighter, one hand caressing down the length of my hair. "I've got you." I let him hold me because it feels good, and because, honestly, no one has held me like this in a really long time. His lips press against the top of my head, his arms not letting me go, his voice soothing as he just keeps telling me I'm okay.

When I feel like I have a handle on my emotions, I move my arms to his chest and push gently to extract myself from him. I peek up under my wet lashes, sniffling. “I’m sorry.”

His brow crinkles as his mouth pulls down. “For what?” He lowers his lips to mine, brushing a tender kiss to them. “For having a nightmare?”

I nod, looking down in an attempt to hide my flaming cheeks. “That hasn’t happened in a long time.” I spin around, searching for that shirt again.

“Hey.” He wraps a hand around my arm, turning me back to face him. “Don’t be sorry. Don’t be embarrassed, and don’t even think about leaving.” He tugs me back into his arms. “Talk to me.”

I chuckle. “I thought I was the shrink.”

“I’m whatever you need me to be.” His voice is strong and calm next to my ear.

“Thank you.” I tighten my embrace around his waist, pressing my body against his. I’m grateful for the comfort he so easily provides to me, especially knowing he has his memories of his own haunting him.

“You don’t have to thank me.” He kisses my tresses again. “Can I get you something? Do you want some tea?”

I lean my head back. “You have tea?”

He chuckles. “I’m not a complete caveman.”

I smile up at him. “I would love some.”

I come out of the bathroom five minutes later, soft gray shirt swishing against my thighs, and scoot myself onto one of the barstools. Patrick’s back is to me as he drops tea bags into two mugs, humming something under his breath as he works. I sweep my gaze over his broad shoulders, his tattoos, the muscles that move each time he shifts his arms. I'm relieved to see the bruises and cuts have healed that splashed across his frame the last time I was here.

He turns around, smirking when he finds me ogling him. "Can I help you with something, ma'am?"

I play with the sugar and milk containers on the counter in front of me, my eyes skimming the length of his torso. He's got a pair of sweats on, hanging loosely on his hips, exposing his defined abs and the light coating of fur on his chest. I lock onto the nipple ring, my tongue sweeping over my lips, then dart my eyes back up to meet his.

He cocks a brow, crossing his arms, his biceps bulging as he does, a chuckle shaking his chest gently. "We can skip the tea."

"I just—" I bite my lip subconsciously then continue. "You have a really nice body."

He glances down at himself then back up at me, his grin turning wicked. "All the better to fuck you with."

"Don't be crude." I laugh, trying to disguise the fact that I would, in fact, like him to fuck me again. The tea kettle whistles behind him, pulling his attention away from me, *thank God*, and he pours the steaming water into the mugs.

He carries them over, places them on the counter in front of us, and sits on the stool next to me. I scoop in a teaspoon of sugar, pour some milk, and then stir the hot liquid. Patrick leaves his as is, taking a small sip from the edge of the cup after blowing on it.

"So, you want to tell me about your dream?" His hand

falls on my knee, his thumb sweeping against the inside of my leg tenderly.

I stare at the space in front of me, avoiding his gaze, absently moving the spoon in a slow circle inside my mug. "I think it's because I talked to my mom today about what happened. It triggered the memories again."

He doesn't say a word, just sips his tea, giving me the time I need to continue.

"It's actually the reason I came to find you today." I glance over at him, cocking my head. "The real reason."

He gives me a small smile, admitting defeat. I spit the words out, knowing every time I say them, it's like a knife piercing my heart. "My father shot himself."

"Jesus." His hand on my knee tightens. "I'm sorry."

I just nod my head and keep going. "I found him. It was awful." I close my eyes, trying to fight back the tears threatening to fall. "There was blood everywhere."

Patrick's arms fold around me and pull me against him. "Stop. You don't have to do this if you don't want to."

I clear my throat and push back from him. "I want to." I bring my gaze up to him. "I need to." I take a sip of the tea, wetting my lips, then continue. "My dad was a captain in the Army." Patrick's brows lift, his mouth gaping open slightly at my revelation. "He was career military, joined when he graduated high school and worked his way up in the ranks." I smile proudly in memory of him. "He had twenty years in and was getting ready to retire, but then, 9-11."

"He re-enlisted," he concludes.

I nod. "He deployed to Afghanistan. I didn't see him for over two years." I turn toward him. "When he came home, he was so different. Withdrawn, moody, no longer the dad who used to hug me ten times a day."

Patrick's eyes shoot down to the counter and away from mine, I'm sure because he understands what I'm describing perfectly.

"He wouldn't talk to anyone. Not my mom. Not a doctor. Certainly not me." I draw a small circle with my finger on the countertop. "And then it was too late for him to talk to anyone because he killed himself."

"I'm not going to kill myself," he says gruffly, swinging my stool so we face each other. "Is that what you think?"

I lock my gaze with his, shaking my head. "No, that's not it." I grip one of his hands in mine. "I talked to my mother today about my dad, about what he went through. What he was feeling. She said something about him that made what you do click into place for me. Or, at least, it helped it make more sense to me."

He nods for me to continue, his fingers entwining through mine in my lap.

"She said that she wished he had some way to deal with the pain. A way to release it, share it, some way to escape his demons." I lean closer to him, my fingers squeezing more tightly around his. "And I realized, if what you do gives you relief, makes you feel less mental pain, makes life more bearable for you, I would rather that for you a thousand times over than what my father did." He goes to speak, but I shake my head to stop him. "And I hate it, Patrick. I can't lie." I look up at him. "I hate that you feel like you need to bleed in order to feel better. That you feel like you have to punish yourself for their deaths. I do. I hate it. But, at least, now, I feel like I understand a little better."

I feel a tear run down my face, and I lift a hand to brush it away, frustrated at my emotions. His lips press against my cheek, tracing the trail of moisture until he finds my mouth, claiming it with his. He pulls back after just a second, lowering his face to mine, capturing my eyes with his. "All I know is that, since you've come into my life, you're what I crave. More than the pain." He leans forward and kisses me again. "You've invaded my thoughts, my senses, pushing the anger and guilt that's consumed me for the last year to the back of my mind."

The therapist in me comes to life, and I blurt what I'm thinking out loud. "You're just trading one obsession for another. How long can that last?"

He scoffs, sitting back. "If it's the lesser of two evils, can it really be that bad?"

"Maybe not for you," I whisper.

He narrows his eyes, leaning even farther back from me, his fingers drumming against the counter. "I would never hurt you."

I sigh. "Not intentionally, Patrick. I know that." I give him a sad smile. "I'm not the kind of woman who sleeps with her patients, or the kind who has casual sex."

"And?" He frowns, his fingers still drumming.

"So, if I'm here, sleeping with you, it means something to me."

"And you think it doesn't to me?" His fingers stop moving as his palm lands flat on the counter.

"Maybe." I look down, my hair falling around my face, hiding my expression. "I don't know."

His fingers reach under my chin, lifting it. "*I* know." He stares at me. "I'm not trading one thing for another. There's something between us, and you know it as well as I do. You feel it as much as I do."

I look back at him, my teeth chewing the skin off my bottom lip, doubt my best friend at the moment.

"You think I only go to that club to punish myself?" He sneers. "I went to that club, other clubs, long before the accident."

My eyes go wide at his revelation. "Oh."

"I've always liked more. Wanted more." He leans closer to me, clenching my thighs in his hands. "Just like you're figuring out you want that, too." He lowers his voice. "It doesn't make it wrong, doesn't make us wrong."

I want to believe him, that what he's feeling for me is so much more than a way to escape his demons.

"Come to the club with me."

"What?" My head swings up, my gaze locking onto his.

"Let me show you that it's not all about punishment or atoning for my sins. Let me prove to you that what I do there isn't just about making me forget. It's about letting me feel, too. I can make you feel so much fucking better than you can even imagine."

My pulse quickens when I think about what a single spanking did to me, excitement and curiosity surging through me. I stare at him, my mouth open, my voice silent.

"Is it wrong that, after a year, I've finally found someone who makes life more bearable? That I feel like maybe I didn't die for a reason? And that, maybe, just maybe, it's okay to forgive myself to try to move forward?" He shakes his head. "'Cause that's what I'm trying to do here, and I only want to do it with you."

"Okay," I breathe out, surrendering to his proposal. Not only because I want so badly for him to feel for me the way I'm beginning to feel for him, but because, more than anything, I want more of what he gave me in that room.

CHAPTER EIGHTEEN

~Trick~

I call Cory at Temptations and ask her to arrange a car for me that evening from the service they use, and then I tell her I'm quitting. I've worked as an escort for over a year, and honestly, have enjoyed it, but know that what I'm feeling for Belle changes everything.

"I kind of thought it was obvious you wouldn't be back when you had me put you on hold a month ago."

"Really?" I'm surprised she would have assumed so easily that I wouldn't return.

"This was a short-term solution for you, Trick. I knew you'd figure your shit out sooner or later and leave."

I laugh. "I guess you knew before I did then."

"I've been here a long time." She chuckles. "I'm not going to say we aren't going to miss you though. You're one of our most popular requests for an escort."

"How's Gabby doing?" I inquire. I referred her to Temptations and was curious how she had been with the clients.

"You didn't hear?" she replies. "She was fired yesterday. We found out she was arrested several weeks ago for propositioning an undercover cop. You know we can't have that associated with the business."

"Fuck." I run a hand down my face as I look up at the ceiling. That's why she showed up at my place drunk last night. "I'll call her."

"She doesn't belong here either." Cory sighs. "So, it was probably a blessing in disguise."

"Yeah, maybe." I frown, feeling like shit now about the way I treated her the night before. "Okay, thanks for everything, Cory."

I hit end on the brand new iPhone I purchased this morning as I stride out of my apartment, using the stairwell to go down one floor. I exit into the hallway, knock on the third door, and wait to see if anyone is home at Trey's place. The door opens after a minute, Trey standing before me, hair tousled and exhausted looking.

"Fuck, you look like hammered shit." I walk inside, not waiting to be invited, the door closing behind me.

"Come on in." He yawns sarcastically. "Want a coffee? I didn't get in 'til after four this morning."

I move to the kitchen. "I'll make it." I motion for him to sit. "Take a load off."

"Who the fuck are you, and what have you done to my friend Trick?" he asks, brows raised in shock as he sits at the breakfast bar.

"Shut up." I sneer at him. "I made coffee all the time

when we lived together." I shove a pod into the Keurig and place a mug under the dispenser, pressing the large cup brew button.

"Not this willingly." He scratches his head, yawning again. "What's going on?"

I pull the cup out and slide it in front of him, leaning over the counter, resting on my forearms. I know he likes it black. "Charlie home?"

He shakes his head. "Hospital." He takes a sip of the coffee, eyes rolling to the back of his head as he hums appreciatively. "Working 'til seven."

"Should she still be working?" I ask, referring to her pregnancy.

"She's not sick, asshole. She's having a baby."

"Yeah, I know, but she's like, getting huge." I lift my shoulders in defense. "It can't be good for her to be on her feet all day."

"She's fine." He gives me a crooked smile. "She's got another seven weeks to go. She'll know when it's too much for her."

"Okay." I shrug. "So, you hear anything about what happened with Gabby?"

"Only a little."

"Cory said she got arrested, and fired, for propositioning a cop."

Trey chokes on the coffee he's just inhaled, his eyes wide when he stops coughing. "What? I sure as hell didn't hear that."

I turn to the sink, tear a paper towel off the roll, then hand it to him. "What did you hear?"

"Charlotte said Gabby got in a fight with Cameron, made a scene at your place, and then cooled off here for a few hours before she put her in a taxi home."

"Well, something sure as hell happened, but I guess we'll have to wait until Charlie gets home to find out all the details." I take the dirty paper towel and throw it away for him. "You working tonight, too?"

He shakes his head. "Nope, we're both off. We're ordering Chinese and going to Netflix and chill."

"Can you do me a favor then?"

"Maybe," he scoffs back, never knowing what to expect from me.

"Can you watch Kane tonight? I'm going out, and I'm not sure when I'll be back." I shake my head in disgust. "I can't believe I'm asking you to fucking babysit."

"Not if it's so you can get a fresh beating down at that damn club," he states, his eyes narrowing in anger.

"Fuck you," I bite out. "I have a date."

"A Temptations date, or a real date?"

"A date. I quit the agency this morning."

His brow quirks up, his jaw dropping. "No fucking way." He shakes his head. "I don't believe it." Then he shoots his gaze up to mine. "Is it the girl? The one Charlotte said you were getting cozy with at the ball?"

"Can you watch the dog or not?" I quip back.

"Yeah, yeah, I'll watch the dog." He slides his cup over to me. "Make me another, will ya?"

I scowl. "Sure, boss."

"So, you going to tell me her name?"

I knew I'd get the fifth degree as soon as I admitted I

have a date with someone. I just expected it to be from Charlie, not him. I make myself busy preparing another coffee for him, keeping silent while I do, letting him wonder. When it's done, I slide it back in front of him. "I'll bring the puppy down around six."

I walk around the counter and toward the exit.

"You're seriously not going to tell me anything?" He huffs. "You're an asshole."

I stop, grinning at him. "Yep." I flip him the finger and keep walking. "Her name's Annabelle Murphy, she's a doctor, and yes, she's legal." I stroll through the door, slamming it behind me before he can ask me anything else.

At exactly seven o'clock, I knock on Belle's door, dressed in a dark gray Tom Ford suit, a white dress shirt, and carrying a bouquet of red roses. When the door swings wide, I let out a long whistle, riveted by the vision that stands before me. I told her to put on a nice dress and some make-up, but she's outdone my wildest fantasy.

She's wearing a stunning bandage style dress, sleeveless with a deep V-neck, exposing the soft, silky skin of her cleavage. The skirt falls to just above her knee, but the last six inches is fringed, showing off a teasing amount of leg when she moves. The silver color of the material highlights the blue of her eyes, which sparkle as she looks back at me.

"Wow." I step up to her, kissing her cheek, my nostrils flaring at her scent. It's musky with undertones of citrus and vanilla, and I want to nuzzle my nose against her neck to inhale again, but I step back and hand her the flowers. "You look stunning."

"Thank you." Her cheeks flush as they rise up in an adorable smile before she buries her nose in the fresh blooms. "These smell divine." She lifts her face, beaming, and takes a step back. "Come in."

I enter, sweeping my gaze around the room, my cock twitching at the memory of her sucking my cock right where I'm standing. I adjust my jacket over my waist and follow her into the small kitchen. She sets the flowers on the counter and opens a cabinet, standing up on her tip-toes for a vase. I reach up behind her, grabbing it easily, and lower it to the counter for her, making sure to inhale deeply as I do, savoring her perfume. "You smell amazing."

She spins around, her body almost flush with mine, her eyes locking with mine. "It's Burberry."

"It's all I ever want to smell on you again." I respond huskily, leaning into her hair, smooth and sleek down her back instead of the usual waves she has, nipping lightly against her ear.

"Patrick," she moans. "We're not going to go anywhere if you don't stop that."

I grumble and step away, knowing she's correct.

"Do you want a drink, or do we have to get to the club straight away?" She fills the vase with water, moving to unwrap the flowers from their packaging.

"I'm fine, thanks." I crumble up the paper as she arranges the flowers. "We're not going to the club tonight though."

Her fingers still on the stems, and she glances up at me. Is it wrong that I'm thrilled to see disappointment on her face? "We're not?"

I shake my head, taking one of her hands in mine, and raise it to my lips, kissing her knuckles. "We're not."

"Then what?" she wonders aloud.

"I'm taking you to dinner. I think a real date is in order before I completely debase and ruin you for all other men."

Her brow arches high. "You think that's what you're going to do to me?"

I lean down, tugging her against my body, and make sure she feels how I react whenever I'm near her. A small gasp escapes her lips. "I hope, when I'm done with you, you'll never look at another man again."

Her head tilts slowly up until her eyes lock with mine, her tongue sweeping across her lips. I flick my tongue out and caress it against hers, crushing my mouth to hers, claiming her the only way I can for now. When I break away, she's panting, her nipples peaked beneath her dress.

It takes all my willpower not to throw her up on the counter. But I walk away instead, pulling her behind me toward the door. "I have a car waiting. Do you have a jacket I can help you with?"

She nods, still dazed from our passionate exchange, and points to the couch. I walk over, stopping when I notice there's a gray ball of fluff curled up on her jacket. "Um, Belle?" I motion to the cat, unsure what to do.

"Nyla!" she exclaims, walking over, her tongue clucking in disapproval. "Get off my jacket, you little fur ball." She lifts it off her jacket, shooing the cat when it strikes a clawed paw at her. She glances over at me. "Meet Nyla, my territorial roommate."

I chuckle. "Hey, at least your coat's in one piece." I shake my head. "You don't even want to know what Kane did to my two-hundred-dollar running shoes."

"Get a pet, they said," she mocks. "It will be fun, they said."

We both laugh, and I help her into her jacket. After opening the door for her, I lead her to the waiting car, more excited to spend time with someone than I can ever remember.

CHAPTER NINETEEN

~Annabelle~

I'd be lying to myself if I didn't admit I'm a little disappointed we aren't going to the club. All day, I wondered what he would do to me. If I would like it. Would he want me to do something to him? Not that I didn't mind spending time with him. I'm every bit as surprised and pleased that he thinks bringing me on a date first will be more appropriate. It shows a side to him I wasn't expecting.

He helps me into a waiting town car then walks around, sliding in next to me, his hand settling possessively on my knee. I study his hands, never really noticing before how long his fingers are or the faint scars that line the back of one hand. Burns from the accident, I wonder?

I trail my eyes appraisingly over the rest of him. His suit is obviously tailored, fitting him perfectly and accentuating every firm muscle on his body. I close my eyes, turning my head toward the window before opening them, still a little shocked that I'm actually sitting here next to a man who was my patient two weeks ago.

"What's wrong?" he questions beside me.

I turn back to him and offer a smile. "Absolutely nothing."

"You're thinking again," he muses.

"Only about how I ended up here with you." I place my hand over his. "It seems a bit like a dream. How quickly things can change in one's life."

He shrugs. "For the better, I hope. For both of us."

I hum, my lips pressed together as I digest what he's said. "Where are you taking me?" I change the subject to something safer.

"One if by Land, Two if by Sea. It's in the village."

"That's a really nice restaurant," I say, my voice raised a little in surprise.

He smirks down at me. "Which is why I asked you to wear a nice dress."

"Can I ask you something?"

"Anything." His eyes fix on mine. "That's why were on a date, so we can get to know each other." He offers me another crooked grin.

"Are you rich? I mean—" I stutter, embarrassed that I'm even asking him this question, because it doesn't matter to me at all if he is or isn't. "I guess, I'm just wondering, because you don't work, or at the very least, maybe are getting disability from the Army. But you live in an amazing apartment, have a car driving us around, and wear tuxedos and suits that cost thousands."

He chuckles, his brows rising as he nods in acknowledgement at all I've just sputtered out. "I'm a little rich, I guess. Yes."

"How?" I slap my hand over my mouth, eliciting a full belly laugh from him. I lower my hand. "Oh my God, I'm so sorry. It's really none of my business."

He places his palm on my cheek, pulling my face to his as he bends, sweeping a kiss across my lips. "You're adorable."

"I'm embarrassed." I place my hand back over my face. "I'm usually not this nosey. I swear."

"I don't mind. Really." He pulls my hand off my face, assuring me. "My grandfather started several shipping companies when he was young. They did very well, and he bought a bunch more. Invested money. Got very rich. When he died, a huge chunk of the money and the business went to my father."

I make eye contact with him, a small frown on my lips as I piece the rest of the puzzle together on my own, even though he continues talking.

"When my parents died, everything my father had went to me." He shrugs. "I'm an only child. When we learned the crash they were in was due to defective equipment on the plane, I was given even more money. It's been sitting in a trust for years."

He wipes a hand down his face, evidence of his discomfort about having all the money obvious. "I honestly don't even know how much I have. My grandmother handles everything for me, and if I need money, I just go to the bank and withdraw some or use one of my credit cards."

He leans his head back against the seat and lets out a loud sigh. "Do I sound like a spoiled, pompous asshole?"

"No! Don't be ridiculous." I grab his hand and squeeze it. "You sound like someone who feels guilty for reaping the benefits of someone else's hard work and misfortune. And you shouldn't. I'm sure your grandfather would be happy to know he has a grandson to share his wealth with. I'm also sure your parents would want to know you were left provided for."

"I do, you know," he says.

"Do what?" I wonder.

"Feel guilty. About having the money." He sits up and looks down at me. "It's why I went to West Point, and then to aviator school. I figured, at the very least, I could give something back to my country."

"And you did." I look back at him, imploring him to believe in himself and the good that he's done.

"Except, I took something away, too." He turns and looks out the window, his voice low. "I took three men away from their families."

I lean forward and grab his face with my hand, pulling it back to look at me. "You didn't take those men away from anyone. Whoever fired that missile, that's who did that." I let go of his face, pointing my finger in anger at him when I continue. "Not you Patrick. Not you!"

He stares at me, his expression void. He finally blinks, his nostrils flaring as he bobs his head once. "I know, but it still hurts like hell."

I slide my hand over his cheek and pull him to my mouth.

"I know." And I kiss him, trying to soothe some of the pain he feels over all the loss he's suffered in his life.

"Mr. Connors, we're here." The driver speaks from the front. I slide my lips from Patrick's and look out the window. I didn't even realize the car had stopped.

He gives me a half-smile. "You still want to go to dinner with this sad sack?"

"More than anything," I reply, sliding my hand into his. He squeezes my fingers once quickly then releases my hand to climb out of the car.

The driver has already come around to open the door, so I step out, and Patrick there to meet me as I do. He places my hand in the crook of his elbow and leads me into the restaurant, the serious conversation and mood left behind in the car.

The restaurant is lovely, the food scrumptious, and our conversation nonstop. We talk about where we grew up, our favorite childhood memories, where I went college, first boyfriends and girlfriends, first heartbreaks, favorite colors, movies, and foods. When we leave the restaurant, I not only feel full; I feel richer for the things we've learned about one another.

We climb back in the car, and Patrick puts an arm around me, drawing me up against his frame as we pull into traffic. "Do you want to go dancing, or go for a nightcap somewhere?" He glances down at the heavy watch on his wrist. "It's still early."

What I really want to do is climb onto his lap and run my hands over his beautiful torso, but I keep that to myself. "A drink sounds wonderful."

He drops a kiss against my temple. "Gene, we'll go to the Oak Room at The Plaza, please."

"Yes, sir."

I rest my head against Patrick's shoulder, relaxing as I watch the sights in the city as we drive up Third Avenue. We ride comfortably in silence, so many things already shared between us this evening that conversation doesn't feel necessary. When we reach The Plaza, we exit the car and head into the luxuriousness of The Oak Room. It's everything you would expect it to be. Warm, dark colored wood tables and bars, low Tiffany lighting, and music coming from a grand piano as we enter.

Patrick speaks to the host, who shows us to a booth tucked into a quiet corner behind the piano, giving us a view of the entire bar. He slides my coat off my shoulders and drapes it over the back of a chair across from us before sitting beside me. A waiter appears in seconds and takes our drink orders. An old fashioned for Patrick, and a pinot noir for me.

"This is nice," I state, glancing around the grand room.

"It's quiet." He gleams down at me, settling his hand on my bare thigh. "And private."

Heat pools in my stomach as his fingers brush back and forth on the inside of my leg. I decide two can play this game and lean into him. I rest my hand just shy of his groin, sliding it up until I bump against his length, glide in the opposite direction, and then back again.

He quirks a brow as he lowers his gaze to mine. "You're playing with fire."

"Maybe I want to get burned," I confess, moving my

hand even higher this time, dragging my fingers heavily down his hard length when I pull back.

He lowers his lips, hissing against my hair, hot air whooshing against my ear. "I will take you into the bathroom and fuck you if you don't stop."

I swing my eyes to his, the green irises dark and glaring in warning. I lick my lips then push them against his, sliding my hand away from his cock, biting onto his lower lip before I release him. "You will fuck me tonight, Patrick Connors. It just won't be here."

His fingers stop brushing against my leg, his grip tightening, his eyes crinkling when his cheeks rise in a devilish grin. "Be careful what you wish for." And then he leans down and pulls my lip between his teeth, returning the bite I just gave him. He pulls away just as the waiter approaches and sets our drinks in front of us.

"Thank you," Patrick says smoothly, giving no indication whatsoever that what just transpired between us affects him.

"How do you do that?" I ask, after the waiter leaves, bringing the wine glass to my lips. I sip the dark burgundy liquid, humming in appreciation of its warm, blackberry flavor.

"Do what?" He fingers the tumbler on the table before raising it to his nose to sniff it, and then casually drinks.

"Act like nothing just happened between us."

He sets the glass on the coaster and takes my hand in his, moving it over his chest before resting it over his heart. I can feel it racing under my palm, it's rhythm erratic and thumping. I sweep my eyes to his, my mouth opening slightly as I gape up at him.

"Don't take everything you see at face value." He bends, brushing a kiss across my open lips. "I figured you already knew that one, Doc."

"I guess I'm not as smart as you think I am," I drawl out.

He chuckles, taking another sip of his drink. I pull my hand off his chest, sitting up straight to also take a drink of my wine.

"So, I just have one more question for you then." He sips his drink, peering over the rim of his glass at me.

"Yes?" I tilt my head coyly, waiting.

He thumps his glass down on the coaster and looms over me, his face only a fraction from mine, the whiskey from his drink flavoring the air between us when he speaks. "Your place or mine?"

CHAPTER TWENTY

~Trick~

"Yours," she purrs up at me. "Because it's closer and I'm tired of waiting." I raise my hand to flag the waiter for the bill, and twenty minutes later, Gene pulls up in front of my building. I slide out of the car, pulling her quickly behind me, eager to finally be alone with her. When we step into the elevator, the air is filled with so much electricity and sexual tension you could cut it with a knife. My fingers are locked around hers, my pulse thrumming against her wrist, our gazes locked on one another.

"One more minute," I murmur, stroking my thumb over hers. She nods, her lower lip caught between her teeth. The doors to the elevator slide open, and we stride to my apartment, slamming the door behind us. I twirl her around and crush her to my body, crashing my mouth against hers. We are a tangle of limbs, our hands roaming greedily over one another, our moans vibrating together.

I tear away from her and strip her coat off, shedding mine next. I wrap an arm around her and loom over her. Her back arches against my arm as I latch onto her neck, biting and sucking my way down the wide V of her neckline. Her fingers grip the waist of my slacks as she shoves her center against my hard cock and rubs against me. I growl, gripping a handful of her hair in my fist, and yank her away from me, standing straight.

Her blue eyes are wide, darting back and forth wildly as she stares at me, her chest heaving as she pants. I tighten the hold I have on her hair and lower my face above hers. "You sure you want more?"

She nods, eyes flaring wider as she breathes out, "Yes."

I release her, take a step back, and move to unbutton the cuffs on my shirt. She watches me but doesn't say a word as I roll up my sleeves to just before my elbows and then loosen the top two buttons of my shirt.

I take a step toward her and chuckle when she takes one back. "You want me to chase you?" I drawl, stepping to the side of her, ready to grab her if she bolts.

She shakes her head, looking at me over her shoulder. "What are you going to do to me?"

I step behind her, wrapping a hand around each of her shoulders, pushing her forward until the fronts of her legs hit the arm of the couch. I press my lips to her ear. "I'm giving you more." Her body shudders in my arms as I release the hold I have on her shoulders. I skim my fingers down the length of her body until I reach the bottom of her skirt. I grab onto the hem and yank it up above her waist, a short cry coming from her as her body jerks against mine.

Pressing my front tightly against her back, I rub my cock against the seam of her ass, my hands sliding up the front of her dress. My fingers trail over her heightened nipples, and I move my thumb and forefinger together and pinch hard. Her ass thrusts back against my cock, a moan tumbling from her lips in response. I bury my nose in her neck, my lips finding bare skin, and I suck, her knees buckling against my assault.

I flatten my hands against her chest to hold her against me, whispering against her ear again. "You still want more?"

"Patrick," she mewls out, her hand reaching behind me to clutch onto my hip, grasping onto me as she pulls me against her ass. "Don't stop."

My cock swells at her command, and I take one hand and twist her face to me, claiming her mouth in a brutal kiss. I tear my lips from hers, releasing my grip on her long enough to step away. I place one hand on her hip, the other between her shoulder blades, and shove her down over the arm of the couch, splaying her body out before me, her ass in the air.

I growl in appreciation at the curves of her ass, bare before me except for a thin scrap of material strung between her cheeks and a small triangle over her pussy. I can see her panties are wet, the silk darker at her core than anywhere else. I run two fingers over the smooth fabric, pushing against her raised clit as I do, a whimper sounding from her as she wiggles beneath me. I raise my hand and slap it hard against her cheek, no warning. She cries out in surprise, one heeled foot kicking out and almost hitting me. She moves to rise off the couch, but I lean over her, grabbing her hands and clenching them against her lower back.

"Leave them there," I order.

She nods once, panting. "Okay."

I rear my hand back then bring it down in the same spot, pink blooming across her buttock, my dick pounding in response. She cries out.

I growl. "Don't you remember anything that I taught you?"

She nods again, more frantic, searching for my approval. "Yes, sir."

I smile, my hand resting gently on the spot I just slapped, caressing it softly in reward. I drop to my knees, my fingers sliding up to grip onto the edges of her thong, and I pull it down her legs, over her shoes, and off. I skim my knuckles up the calf of her legs, stopping when I get to her knees, gripping them lightly, then pull them wide.

She grunts when her body slides forward but manages to keep her hands clenched behind her back, turning her face sideways. I continue moving my hands up her legs until I reach her ass, then I grip onto each cheek and spread them wide. I lower my face and drag my tongue from the hood of her clit to the top of her ass, swirling my tongue around her puckered hole, repeating the action several times.

"Ooooh," keens from above, her pussy clenching, moisture dripping from her. I lean forward and lap at it, stabbing my tongue deep inside of her, thrusting it back and forth. Her cries above me intensify with every shove. I bring my hand up and sink two fingers inside of her, her legs opening wider as I slowly pump them in and out of her.

She's whimpering above me, her hips grinding into the arm of my couch in time to my thrusts. I lap my tongue over her clit then close my lips around it and suck. I hook my fingers, plunging harder until I feel her pussy begin pulsing, clenching onto my digits with force, her screams of passion bouncing of the walls of the room as she comes against my mouth.

I clamp a hand down hard on her waist as I continue to suck, her juices dripping around my mouth as she convulses against me. I hum as I draw back, licking my lips, standing quickly to unbuckle my belt, and shove my pants down my legs. My cock springs free, my head swollen and aching as I grip it with my fist and line it up against her wet core.

I swipe it up and down her center, spreading her slickness over my head. "Are you ready for more?" I push into her opening, leaning over her as I slide myself slowly into her.

"Oh my God, oh my God, oh my God," falls from her again and again like a chant, her ass grinding back against me, showing me her answer. I lunge forward, shoving myself in to the hilt, a low moan shuddering from her as I bark out my pleasure. "Fuck yes!"

I rear my hips back and then drive them into her again, her body flailing forward when I do. I reach down to grip her wrists in one hand, pushing down to hold her in place. Then I lean over farther, gathering her long hair, wrapping it around my fist, and pull. Her head yanks back at the same time my hips drive into her, her approval wailing from her. "Yes, yes!"

Sweat drips down my back, my shirt sticking to my skin as I ram into her again and again. I fuck her relentlessly until I feel my release coil up my length and explode, the fragments of my mind going with it, shards of lightning sparking behind my closed lids as I roar out her name and collapse against her.

~

I jerk to a sitting position, the heat of the flames still burning against my skin, my heart like a jackhammer against my chest. My body is covered in sweat, the covers twisted around my legs as I blow out a hot breath. *Another fucking nightmare.* I reach down to untangle myself and realize Belle's not in the bed with me. *What the fuck?* I glance at the clock on my bedside table. It's a little after three in the morning. *There's no way she would have left, right?*

I rip my legs out of the covers and out of the bed. I'm naked, but I don't stop to put anything on, more concerned about where she is. I fling the bedroom door open and let out a sigh of relief when I see her sitting on the couch.

"You okay?" I walk to the couch to join her. "I got worried when I woke up and you—" I freeze in my tracks, my eyes locking onto the gun she's holding in her lap—my Glock 19x 9mm, to be precise.

She turns her head to look at me, tears streaming from her eyes. I hold my hand out and walk cautiously over to her. "Belle, what are you doing with that?" I stop when I'm next to her, slowly lowering myself beside her.

She shakes her head, tears streaming down her face, her mouth open, but no words come out. I place my hand over the gun, wrap my fingers around it, then lift it out of hers. I make sure the safety's on, even though I know it's not loaded, then place it on the coffee table in front of us.

"Belle?" I put my palm against her wet cheek and turn her face to look at mine, trying to make some kind of contact. She blinks, seeming to finally realize I'm here, and reaches up to clutch onto my arm.

"Why do you have a gun?" Her eyes dart back and forth as she stares at me, her hands clenching into fists. "Why would you have one here?" she begs.

I raise my shoulders, my brow furrowing. "I'm a soldier." I'm not sure what other explanation to give. I actually have three guns in the apartment, but I'm guessing now isn't the time to reveal that piece of information. And, I'm wondering how she came to find this one. "I was active duty for so long. It's just second nature for me to have one."

She starts rambling, and I rear back as I try to absorb everything she's saying. "I woke up, and I had to go pee. I was cold, so I wanted a t-shirt. It was dark, but I didn't want to turn on the light and wake you, and I was trying to remember where you got that other shirt that you gave me that time. So, I opened what I thought was the correct drawer, but I reached in and my hand landed on this, and oh my God, a gun! Why do you need a gun?"

"Hey." I reach out and take her face in my hands, talking to her in a soft voice. "Belle, it's okay. I'm not your dad. I'm not going to hurt myself. It's not why I have it."

Her eyes fly up to mine, her face scrunched up in pain. "I can't go through that again." She shakes her head. 'I won't." She begins to sob, so I pull her against my chest and hold her, telling her softly that it's okay, and just let her cry.

Jesus Christ, I guess we both have demons breathing down our backs. I would have never imagined seeing a gun would trigger her this way. When her crying finally seems to subside, I shift her onto my lap then stand and carry her back to my bedroom. I set her gently on the bed then slide in next to her, gathering her in my arms to pull her against my chest. I reach down to pull the covers over the both of us when I feel her trembling. I'm not sure if she's cold or if her body is reacting to her emotions, but I just want to make her feel better.

I kiss the top of her head and tug her even closer to me, wanting her to know more than anything that she's safe here with me. But, even more than that, that I'm not going to do anything to harm myself.

"Belle, I would never, ever use that gun on myself." I sigh. "If I can make you believe anything about myself, please, just believe that."

"My mother didn't think my father would ever use his gun on himself either, Patrick," she mumbles, her cheek wet against my chest.

"I am not your father." I blow out a breath, trying to figure out how I can make her believe me. "I've found a way to deal with the pain, the memories, even the guilt. Something you said your father never did."

"But is what you're doing enough, Patrick?" She looks up me, her eyes so sad. "Is it?"

I close my eyes, knowing that some days it doesn't feel like enough. I tell her the truth. "Some days, it fucking sucks. Some days are really hard. The guilt I feel, the pain, they can be overwhelming." I sigh. "But I also know I'd rather feel that pain, feel that guilt, than feel nothing at all or leave behind the people I love."

I pull her far enough away from me that I can look down at her. "I'm sorry your dad did that to himself. I'm sorry he did that to your mom and you. Really sorry." I frown when I see her eyes well up. "But, I promise you, I would never do that to you." I lower my face to hers. "I'll get rid of my guns if you want, but Belle, it wouldn't matter. If I really wanted to do it, I wouldn't need a gun. There are ten other ways I could off myself."

"Is that supposed to make me feel better?" She pushes off of me and sits up. "'Cause it's not working."

Gripping the back of my neck in frustration, I sit up beside her. "No, I'm not saying this right." I grimace. "I would have done it a long time ago if I was going to do it. Not now. Not when I've finally met someone who—" I stop, realizing what I'm about to admit, and just shake my head instead. "I just wouldn't."

"When you finally met someone who, what?" She raises her brows, waving her hand in the air for me to continue.

I lock my gaze with hers, knowing this will either make things better or just scare her away. "When I've finally met someone who makes me feel alive again. Makes me want to get out of bed every morning. Makes me think about what's next."

Her face softens. "Me?"

I scoff. "Of course, you." I haul her against me. "Who else but you?" I press a tender kiss to her lips. "I'm not going anywhere."

CHAPTER TWENTY-ONE

~Annabelle~

I roll over, blinking my eyes, looking for Patrick, but he's not there. I sit up, raise my arms over my head, stretching as I yawn, and glance over at the clock. It's almost ten o'clock. Wow, I can't remember the last time I slept this late, but we were up half the night dealing with my emotional breakdown.

Flopping back onto the bed, I slap my arm over my face and wonder if I can just hide in here for, like, ever. I'm the damn psychiatrist. I'm the one who is supposed to be supporting Patrick. Instead, he's the one helping me discover parts of myself I never knew existed, while also mopping up the pieces of my broken past.

Last night shook me. I hadn't seen a gun since the day I found my father. My reaction was one I didn't expect, but it also made me realize that I have come to feel enough for

Patrick that I'm afraid what might happen if he's no longer here. How many classes did I take about how *not* to fall for your patients?

I groan, knowing I can't hide in here forever, so I sit back up and haul my butt out of the bed. I notice a couple t-shirts on the end of the bed and smile again at Patrick's thoughtfulness. He really is a marshmallow under that hard shell of his. I pick up one of the shirts he left and lift it to my nose. I inhale, my eyes closing when his scent invades my senses. There's nothing better than his smell. I smile as I slide the shirt over my body then exit the room, putting on a brave smile as I do.

"Hey, sleeping beauty." Patrick rises from the stool he's on in front of the breakfast bar and comes to me, wrapping me in an embrace. His lips press against the top of my head and then lower to my mouth. "Good morning." His voice is husky as his eyes scan down my body.

"Morning." I place my palm on his cheek and press my lips to his for another kiss. His hand snakes around my back, grasping onto my ass, pulling me flush to him, his lips dropping against mine again.

"Wanna go back to bed?" he mumbles against my mouth, his hand gliding under the shirt to cup my bare ass.

Before I can answer, Kane starts barking below me, running around my feet, then sinks his pointy little canines into my ankle. I jump, trying not to step on the little shit when I land, and cry out, "Ouch!" I look down at him, hands on my hips. "What the heck was that for?"

Patrick laughs out loud, bending down to scoop him up off the floor. "Yeah, what was that for?" He scrunches up his face as he pretends to be angry at the puppy, talking to him in a baby voice. "You can't go around biting my lover." He looks over at me, arching one brow. "That's my job."

I slap him playfully on his bicep then lean over and mock-snarl at Kane. "You aren't my friend anymore, you little cretin." I give him a 'hmpf' for good measure then stroll away and head to the bathroom. "I'll be right out."

When I exit, Patrick has a steaming cup of coffee in his hands waiting for me. He extends it toward me. "Cream and sugar, right?"

My cheeks rise as my gaze meets his, my hands cupping around the mug. "Yes, thank you." I take a sip. "Yum."

"Are you hungry?" He walks to the other side of the breakfast bar and opens the fridge. "I've got yogurt, some fruit, eggs." He looks back at me over his shoulder.

I slide up onto one of the stools. "Not yet." I put the mug down on the counter. "Thanks though."

He shuts the fridge and turns, leaning against the counter across from me. He looks down at his hands, the tips of his index fingers tapping together, then back up at me. "You okay this morning?"

I feel my cheeks heat, and I stare down at my coffee like it's the most interesting thing in the world, embarrassed to meet his eyes. "I'm really sorry about that."

His fingers stop tapping as he stands straight, placing his palms face down on the counter. "There's nothing to apologize for. I'm the one who's sorry about the gun. Sorry it scared you."

I look up, bringing my eyes to his. "It wasn't the gun as

much as it was the fear of what you could do with it. If that makes sense?"

He doesn't look away from me, nodding his understanding. "You believe what I told you last night, right?"

"I do." I frown, blowing a small breath out between my lips. "But I'm not going to lie and say that I'm still not worried about you. I can't be the answer when it comes to solving all your pain and guilt, Patrick."

He pushes up off the counter and crosses his arms, his stance widening. He does this when he's about to get confrontational. I saw it a dozen times in my office. "I'm not asking you to be."

"Good, because I can't be that for you." I run my finger around the rim of the mug and then continue. "But I do want to be with you, Patrick. You've done something to me. Awakened me somehow. When you look at me, I just—" I gaze up at him, making sure his eyes are on mine. "I never want you to stop."

He moves quickly, coming from around the bar to stand next to me, spinning the stool around so that my legs are between his. He places his hands on the counter behind me and leans in until his face is a few inches from mine. "I'm not sure I could stop looking at you. You've enchanted me, body and soul."

"Patrick," I whisper, bringing my hands up to cup his face, stubble prickling under my palms. "How did we get here so fast?"

"Was it fast?" He chuckles. "I feel like I've been waiting a lifetime."

"I think I'm falling in love with you." I breathe out as he

leans in closer, his eyes closing as he grazes his lips against mine, inhaling deeply as he does.

When he pulls back, his eyes are open, the green of his irises bright as he stares back at me. One side of his mouth quirks up as he barely shakes his head. "I've already fallen." Then his lips melt against mine.

He slides his hands under me, lifting me, and I wrap my legs around him. My bare core rubs against the waistband of his sweats as he carries me to the bedroom. He lays me back on the bed and uses his body to show me just how hard he's fallen.

~

We lie tangled together an hour later, my fingers brushing lazily back and forth over his nipple ring, my absolute favorite accessory ever.

"If you keep doing that, I'm going to roll you onto your back and shove my cock inside your pussy again." His chest rumbles in laughter. "I just wanted to give you fair warning."

My fingers still, and I lay my hand flat, giggling. "Not that I don't love you inside me, but I think I need a break." I giggle again. "And a damn shower."

He lifts his head off the pillow, peering down at me. "Together?"

"Haven't you had enough?" I cry out in mock disbelief.

"No." He skims his fingers over my arm and across one of my nipples. "I'm not sure I'll ever get enough."

I bite my lip, trying to stifle the smile rising on my lips. *How does he know how to say the absolute perfect thing?*

"Keep saying things like that, Patrick Connors, and I'll never leave your bed."

He rolls over on top of me, grinning down at me. "Good." He drops a peck on my nose then my lips. "Are you hungry? 'Cause I'm fucking starving."

I laugh out loud. Men and their stomachs. "I could eat." I cock my head under him. "After a shower though."

He jumps off of me and stands beside the bed. He reaches a hand out, grabbing mine, and pulls me up and out of the bed.

I frown. "Crap."

"What?"

"All I have to wear is my dress from last night." I scrunch my nose up, not wanting to slide back into that after I shower.

"I have an idea." He reaches to the floor for his sweats, slides them on, then pulls the t-shirt I was wearing before over his head. "Wait here." He plops a kiss on my lips. "I'll be right back."

He's gone before I can reply, the door slamming behind him as he exits the apartment. "Where the hell is he going?" I look over at Kane, who's sitting on the couch, looking over at me like he's wondering the same thing.

I pull on the other t-shirt he had left earlier for me on the end of the bed. I walk over and plop down beside Kane, his little body bouncing when I land, his ears popping up. I laugh. "That's for biting me, you little shark." I pull him onto my lap and rub him affectionately behind the ears, his cuteness making it impossible not to forgive him. He's still snuggled on my lap when Patrick returns a few minutes later.

He strides through the door with his hands full. "Okay, I got yoga pants, a sweatshirt, a dress, a pair of jeans, a couple t-shirts, a pair of sneakers, and a pair of flip-flops in case the sneakers don't fit." He raises his brows. "I didn't know your shoe size."

"I'm a seven." I rise from the couch, putting the puppy on the floor, then start rifling through the pile of clothing he's holding in his hands. "Where in the world did you get this?"

"Charlie." He transfers the pile from his arms to mine. "She's not using any of this right now 'cause she's so preggers." He scans me from head to toe. "You're a little curvier, but basically, you look to be about the same size."

I arch a brow. "Curvier? Is that a polite way of saying something else?"

"What?" He grabs me, yanking me against him, the clothes in my arms squished between us. "You've got the most amazing body I've ever laid eyes on." He smashes his mouth against mine then smacks his hand once against my ass. "I'll take you in the bedroom right now if you want me to prove it to you." He grins wickedly.

I giggle. "No, I'm satisfied with your reply." I push him away, smiling, then move to the couch so I can better inspect what he's brought me. "Are you sure Charlie doesn't mind me wearing any of this?"

"Positive." He walks over and sits on the couch, watching me sort through the clothes. "She's the one who gave it to me, with the condition that we come to dinner tomorrow so she can meet you." He clenches his teeth together, his lips curled back, as he waits for my reply.

"Sure you won't be sick of me by then?" I joke.

He grabs me by the waist and swings me over his lap, a screech sounding from me as I land. One hand clamps down on my back while the other raises the bottom of the t-shirt I'm wearing, exposing my bare ass. He places his hand flat on one of my cheeks and begins rubbing it in a soft, small circle. "I thought I already made it clear that I would never get enough of you?"

I peek up over my shoulder at him, wondering what he's going to do to me. I keep waiting for him to raise his hand and bring it down against my skin, but instead, he just keeps caressing me, his hand making wider and wider circles, his fingers skimming so low they tease against my pussy.

I know I told him I needed a break, but apparently, my body has other ideas. My core throbs every time his fingers swipe against me, warmth spreading over my body with every stroke. I whimper the next time he brushes against my lips, and I push myself back, trying to force his fingers against me.

My ass feels momentarily cool when his hand lifts, then flaming hot when that hand slaps hard against my pussy. I wail in pleasure when my core convulses tightly, my fingers digging into the pile of clothes on the couch.

His voice drawls heatedly against my ear as he bends over me. "How am I supposed to punish you," his hand smacks against my pussy again, and I mewl out in pleasure as it pulses again, "when you like this entirely too much?" He fists my hair in his grip and pulls my mouth up to his, a chuckle vibrating up from his chest as he shoves his mouth against mine.

I can feel his cock throbbing against my belly, and I

squirm, wanting him to feel as needy as I do. He rips his mouth from mine, releasing his hold on my head, and presses his hand against my back again so I can't move. "Oh, no, you don't." His other hand comes down hard again on my pussy, and I groan long and loud, certain I'm going to come any moment.

He slides a finger down my slit, pushing it inside my opening, another moan rolling out of my mouth when he pumps it excruciatingly slowly in then out of me. I feel myself begin to quicken then tighten around his finger and close my eyes, so ready for the wave to carry me over the edge. Instead, he slides his finger out and then swings me off his lap into a sitting position beside him, my mouth falling open in a large O.

He slides his finger into his mouth and sucks, his cheeks puckering, a pop sounding when it pulls free. One side of his mouth cocks up in a wicked grin. "That's how I punish you." He tilts his head, a cocky smile still smeared his face. "Now, you know what it feels like to me be. Always wanting." He leans forward and sweeps his tongue over my still gaping mouth, chuckling evilly. "I'm gonna go take a shower." Then he stands and leaves me on the couch, desire coursing through me.

CHAPTER TWENTY-TWO

~Trick~

I smile when Belle walks out of the bathroom and twirls in a small circle. She wearing a pair of black yoga pants with a NYU hoodie, her hair pulled up on top of her head in a long, wavy ponytail. She's not wearing any makeup, and I honestly believe she could pass for a college student. She's got the white chucks on, a pair of my socks helping to supplement the half size too large the sneakers are.

"You look great." I pull her into a hug and plant a kiss against her cheek. "I want to show you something before we go, okay?"

She nods. "okay."

I take her hand and lead her over to the coffee table. She

halts, her arm yanking me to a stop. I turn my head to her. "Just come here. I need to show you this. It's important."

Her eyes are locked on the three handguns sitting on the table. I took them out while she was in the shower. She allows me to shuffle her to the couch, where she drops down, her eyes still locked on the weapons.

I pick up the gun she found last night and cock it, exposing the chamber to her. "This is empty, see?" I click the release for the magazine, catching it as it drops. I hold it up for her. "This is empty, too."

I point to the other guns on the table. "Those are all empty, too." I turn my gaze to her, making sure to make eye contact with her. "I'd never keep a loaded weapon in the apartment."

She blinks. I push and lock the magazine back into the Glock then set it on the table. I grab her hand and pull her back up. "Come."

I lead her through my bedroom, opening the door to my closet, and step inside. I point to a large safe I have against the wall. "That's where I normally keep my guns." I let go of her hand and key in the combination on the number pad, unlocking the safe, then crank the door wide. I reach in and extract a small lock box and set it on top of the safe. I turn and look at it, motioning for her to come closer. "Come here."

She takes two tentative steps to stand beside me. "The ammunition for each gun, as well as loaded magazines, are locked in here." I look down at her. "Completely separate from the gun. Only taken out if I'm going to the range."

She nods, her teeth gnawing on her lower lip, eyes

darting nervously around the closet. I let out a sigh and turn to her. "Belle, it's important for you to understand that I adhere to every gun safety rule I can think of. I don't want you to feel uncomfortable when you're here. Tell me what else I can do to prove that to you."

"Why do you need them at all?" Her voice is low.

I think about her a question for a minute. "I guess I really don't." I shrug. "My father was a soldier, and then so was I, heading to military school right after high school. I suppose it's a part of my identity, almost second nature to me. I don't even really think about the why, if I'm really honest."

"But you understand why it makes me uncomfortable." She looks up at me.

"Of course." I rest a hand on her shoulder. "Which is why I'm showing this to you, so you know." I bend down so I can look her straight in the eye. "You're safe, and I'm safe. I'm never going to use them for anything other than target practice anymore. But if that's not enough for you, I'll get rid of them. I'll go lock them up at my grandmother's house."

She steps forward and slides her arms around my back, resting her head against my shoulder, hugging me tightly. "Just lock them up. I don't want to see them." She lifts her head to look at me. "But I trust you."

I press my lips against hers, my hands cupping her face, then pull away. "Thank you."

She blinks, her lips tilting up in the faintest smile, and nods. "Thank you for understanding."

We separate then, and I take a few minutes to put the guns back in the safe, along with the lock box, and secure them inside. I meet her back in the living room where she's packed her dress and shoes into one of my canvas shopping bags.

"You ready to eat?" I ask, walking over to her, dropping a kiss on the top of her head above her ponytail.

"Yep. Do you want to take Kane?" She looks down at the little rug rat, pouncing on our feet again.

"You okay with that?" I bend down and pick him up.

"Of course." She kisses him on the nose, his tongue sliding out to lap against her nose, causing a laugh to erupt from her.

I grab his leash while she finds her little purse from last night, and we leave, making our way downstairs and out into the street. I put the puppy down on the ground, and we start strolling hand in hand down the sidewalk. It's gorgeous out. It has to be at least sixty-five degrees, and I comment that spring has finally arrived.

"Can we swing by my place after we eat so I can check on Nyla and grab something of my own to wear?"

"Sure." I nod, tugging on Kane's leash, prompting him to walk. He stops and smells every single thing along the way.

We find a restaurant that has some outdoor seating set up, so we stop and ask for a table. We're seated immediately, and Kane plops down under the table, his head resting between his paws.

A waitress comes over and takes our drink order before handing us each a menu. When she returns, she even has a small bowl of water for Kane, and I realize it's things like this that make me love living in this city. Kindness happens at the most unexpected of times and places. We order, me a burger and fries, her a grilled cheese and tomato soup.

"So, I had a thought earlier, but I don't want to get too shrinky on you." She brings her fingers up, making quotation marks in the air when she says shrinky.

"Okay," I grunt out, not sure I want to hear this. I feel like we've finally gotten to a place of acceptance with each other.

"I have a friend who opened a gym for veterans over in the Warehouse District. He lost part of his leg over in Afghanistan and had a really hard time when he got back. He actually did try to commit suicide." She pauses, clearing her throat. "Luckily, he survived. And he got to a place where he wanted to find a way to help people coming back from combat or from being deployed, who may be suffering and need an outlet."

She takes another drink from her glass, continuing when I don't say anything. "Anyway, the guy is Benjamin Sapphire. You may have heard of him. He and his brother own all the Sapphire resorts."

I take a slug out of my beer. "I know who the Sapphires are. I've been to events with my grandmother that they've been at. But I haven't heard of the gym."

The waitress brings our food, interrupting our conversation for just a minute to make sure we're all set, then leaves us to eat. I take a chunk out of my burger and watch as Belle dips a corner of her sandwich into her soup then bites into it delicately. We couldn't be more opposite in our eating habits, and I wonder if perhaps her *Beauty and the Beast* reference really isn't inappropriate.

She swallows and continues. "So, anyway, Ben's gym, it's free to anyone who's served in any branch of the military. They have boxing, every kind of weight training you can imagine, and I think a couple different kinds of martial arts classes."

"You want me to go to a gym?" I scoff and take another long pull from my beer, motioning for the waitress to bring me another. "I already belong to a gym."

"He has a mental health staff there as well," she adds quickly, her eyes darting to mine and then back to her food. "I think you need to talk to someone. And, let's face it, traditional therapy isn't working for you." She picks up her spoon and takes a small sip of the soup then puts it back down. "And that's free, too."

"I think we've established money isn't a problem for me." I take the new beer the waitress hands me and take a long drink. I know I'm being a bit of a dick right now, but I'm kind of pissed. Maybe it's partly because this reminds me of appointments in her office, and I thought I was going out to have a lunch with her, not have a fucking session.

She frowns. "I know that." She taps her fingers on the table. "I think being around other soldiers who have been through the same types of things as you would be helpful. You would be among those who understand better than anyone else what you've experienced. And, maybe, just maybe, you can step into a ring and let someone beat the shit out of you there, instead of at that club." Her voice rises slightly at the end in anger.

My brows shoot up as I realize why she really wants me to go to the gym. She's worried about whether or not she's going to be enough for me, and if I'm still going to need to go find that somewhere else. I can't blame her for worrying about that. Shit, the last few times I went to the club, I had been to be beaten, and it was because I felt like I deserved it. Deserved to be punished for living, because they weren't. But it wasn't the only reason I went. I didn't always go to that part of the club. Above and beyond the beatings, I liked my sex rough and hard. I liked being in control, my partner at my mercy. But just being with her over the last two weeks has shown me that she can give me that and so much more.

Now, I have to try to make sure she realizes this. That being with her gives me so much more than I ever could hope to receive at the club, because, fuck, I'm in love with her. If going to this gym helps prove to her that she's enough, then I'll do that for her.

"Okay."

Her eyes jump up to mine, open wide. "Really?"

I nod. "If you think it will help, I'll go and meet Ben."

"Why?" She narrows her eyes. "You've barely put up a fight."

I chuckle. She already knows me better than she thinks. "Because it's important to you, and I want you to know that you're enough. I don't need to go to the club, Belle. Not anymore. Not if it makes you think less of me."

Her hand reaches out and grabs onto mine, her head shaking. "Not less, Patrick. Never." She laces her fingers into mine. "You've suffered a loss in a way I can't even fathom. But you need to forgive yourself for what happened, and you need to stop feeling like you deserve to be punished for still being here when they aren't. Can you honestly tell me any of the men you served with would have wanted that?"

I frown, drawing my brows together as I think about that. Our job was always to have each other's backs. Serve for one another. One for all and all for one. And, now, I'm the only one left. "I honestly don't know the answer to that, Doc."

"Well, maybe being around other soldiers will help you figure that out."

"Maybe." I look down at our hands and then back up at her. "If nothing else, it brought me to you. That's honestly the best thing that's ever happened to me."

Her face softens, and she shakes her head gently. "And there you go saying the most perfect thing to me again." She smiles and shrugs. "How the hell am I not supposed to fall in love with you when you say stuff like that?"

"Just go ahead and fall." I give her a lopsided grin. "You can keep me company."

Her cheeks rise as her smile blooms wide, her blue eyes sparkling, her fingers tightening around mine.

"We done with the *shrinky* stuff?" I smirk. "Can we get back to the sexy stuff, like going back to your apartment so I can watch you change and see what kind of underwear I'll get to rip off you later?"

She swipes her hand across the air in front of us. "I'm done. No more shrink stuff today. I promise."

CHAPTER TWENTY-THREE

~Annabelle~

We finish lunch and decide to walk the twelve blocks to my place because it's just too nice out not to enjoy some of the day. What would have normally taken us thirty minutes, takes over an hour, Kane investigating every nook and cranny along the way. I don't mind. Patrick keeps my fingers caged securely in his, his dominant nature making me feel safe and possessed in the best of possible ways.

When we reach my place, there's an unexpected battle of wills when Kane discovers Nyla and chases her throughout the apartment. Kane finally gives up when Nyla escapes to the top of my dresser, knocking over several perfume bottles in the process, height her new best friend. She hisses when I go over and try to soothe her, clearly not impressed with my visitors.

"Well, this could be a problem." Trick chuckles, scratching his chin after the entire chaotic scene is over. He's got Kane securely gathered in his lap, panting like he just ran the marathon.

"Ya think?" I chide back. I point at the cat and lift my arms in the air. "I mean, holy shit. What am I supposed to do with that ball of fury right there?"

He frowns, nodding. "Especially if we end up living together."

Whoa! Did he just say what I think he said? My head whips in his direction as I digest the meaning of his words. Something I hadn't even gotten far enough in my thinking to consider yet. "Um, yeah, I think we're a little way off before we have to worry about that."

His brows arch up in surprise. He slides the puppy off his lap onto the couch and moves to come stand in front of me. "I didn't mean tomorrow, Belle, but I guess I thought we were on the same page."

"We are." I place my hand flat on his chest. It falls right over his hoop, and I inwardly curse my body when heat surges through my veins. I continue, stammering. "But, I mean, we've only spent two nights together. I thought we were still in the getting to know you phase. I didn't think we were at a stage where we have to worry about our pets cohabitating."

His eyes bore down into mine, the edges dark as they narrow. He's silent for a moment then scoffs, shaking his head as he walks back to the couch. "Whatever. If that's what you *think*."

My mouth gapes open, my mind spinning at his reaction. "You're kidding, right?" I stomp over, jamming my hands on my hips as I stand over him.

He glares right back up at me, practically snarling at me. "Whatever makes *you* comfortable, Belle."

"What is your god damn problem?" I raise my hands as I ask the question. "You seriously didn't think we were going to be moving in together after two weeks?"

He stands abruptly, towering over me, his jaw clenched as he speaks. "I honestly hadn't even thought about it until the pets from hell scene just unfolded. But seeing how strong your reaction is to even the suggestion of it says everything I need to know about how you feel."

"Patrick," I start, my hands landing on my hips again. "It's been two weeks. *Two*. You really want to talk about this now? Already?"

His chin rocks back and forth as his jaw clenches, his nostrils flaring as he breaths down at me. "Nine weeks," he drawls out in a hot breath. "Seventy-one days. That's how long I've known you, how long I've known you were different. Seventy-one days since I walked into your office, and my heart fucking stopped in my chest at the sight of you."

What? I stare at him, unable to find any words at his revelation. I know he said he'd fallen for me, but I had no idea how long he had been feeling that much for me. I'm literally dumbstruck, my head trying to rationalize what he's saying to me.

He steps to the side, away from me, his hand raking through his hair. "You know how I feel, Belle." He reaches down to pick Kane off the couch, turning to me. "Figure out what you want."

He strides to the door, pulling it open, the fact that he's leaving finally triggering a reaction from me. "Patrick, wait!" I scurry toward him.

He looks over his shoulder at me, his face stoic. "I've been waiting my whole god damn life for you, and I didn't even know it." His lips press firmly together as a second ticks by. "I'm done waiting." He breaks my gaze then storms out.

I flinch as the door slams shut, my hand stretched out to him, but it's too late. *What in the hell just happened?* I lower my arm, still staring at the door, my feet planted in place, not sure what I should do. Give him space? Go after him? Scream in frustration? We went from zero to sixty in five minutes flat.

I jump when the cat rubs against my leg. At least, one of us is happy that Patrick left. I push her away with my foot, scowling down at her. "Thanks a lot, you little trouble-maker." That's right, I'm blaming the cat for what just happened. It certainly isn't my fault. Or is it? I walk absently over to a chair and sink into in, replaying the entire event in my head. Did I overreact? Did he?

"Ugh!" I yell, shooting up, then stomping over to my phone. I need a second opinion. I find my phone and text for back-up, telling Krystal and Holly we need an emergency wine-infused meeting at my place. They respond almost immediately, both of them letting me know they'll be here in an hour.

Sure enough, an hour later, both girls show up on my doorstep, jumbo bottles of wine in hand, coming to my rescue. Ten minutes later, we're situated comfortably in my living room, glasses in hand, and I tell them everything. I tell them about the ball, coming back to my apartment, the blow-job—'cause yes, we're girls and we share stuff like that. I also tell them about the marks on his back and how he likes pain, a lot of pain, and how much that scares me because I know it's not something I can do to him.

I explain to them my mini-epiphany about my dad's suicide and how what Patrick does at the club actually provides him some kind of salvation from the pain that my father couldn't or wasn't able to find. I tell them about going to him at his place, the exceptional sex, the date he took me on, and the even better sex. Right up until this afternoon when I may have screwed everything up when he mentioned us moving in together.

"Do you love him?" Holly asks, never one to mince words.

"I don't know." I take a big gulp of my wine, needing to catch up with the girls since I've been yammering on for the past fifteen minutes. "I like him. A lot."

"That's it?" Holly declares, not satisfied. "You like him a lot?"

"I mean, Jesus, the sex is incredible." I look up at them both, giggling, my cheeks flaming as I admit the next truth. "I want to climb him like a tree every damn second I'm with him, and you both know that I've never even liked sex that much."

"That's 'cause you obviously weren't doing it right," Holly states, raising her glass in the air to confirm her wisdom.

"Or because, now, you're doing it with the right person," Krystal concludes, bringing me right back to my problem.

"I like him, you guys," I groan. "I really like him." I give them a pleading look. "But I mean, technically, we've been dating, if you can even call it that, two weeks. Can you even fall in love in two weeks? Decide you want to be with someone in two weeks?"

Holly and Krystal simultaneously nod and speak in unison, "Yes."

Krystal speaks first. "There's no time limit to how long it should take someone to fall in love, Belle. You of all people should know that there aren't any hard and fast rules around how emotions work. For some people, it's two days, some two months, some two years. Stop letting your brain do all your thinking for you, and for once, just follow your heart."

Holly purses her lips up in a smile, nodding. "Yep, what she said."

"But, you guys, he's kind of a mess."

Holly cocks her head, her brow quirked high. "Isn't that the pot calling the kettle black, girl? I mean, you're not exactly the poster child for your typical, happy-go-lucky kind of girl either."

"I'm happy!" I defend.

They both stare back at me then shake their heads. "Um, no. Coming home every night to this," Krystal waves her hand in a circle around the room, "your cat and a bottle of wine, after talking to depressed soldiers all day? Add not dating or getting laid for a year, and that is not what I describe as happy."

"*Ten months*!" I bang my fist on the arm of the chair I'm

sitting in, then I break into a wide grin. "Actually, it's only been like," I look up at the clock on my wall, "six hours."

We all start laughing, breaking the tension that had been building in the room. When we calm down, I take a sip of my wine and shrug. "Did I totally mess things up?"

"No," Holly soothes. "It's a lot in a really short amount of time."

"Just give him some time to understand your point of view and to cool down a little," Krystal chimes in. "He said he loves you." She gives me a small smile. "If he really does, he's not going to give up that easily."

"Is it weird that I already miss him?" I curl one side of my mouth down.

"You love him," Holly declares.

"Holly!" I admonish.

"You're not denying it," she teases me back.

I hide my smile behind my glass as I take another chug of my wine, unable to admit out loud that she's right. I have fallen in love with him—maybe as long ago as my first meeting with him, which would explain why I never treated him the same as I did my other patients. Because he isn't the same. I just could never admit it to myself, because I always felt I had to follow the rules of logic instead of the rules of the heart.

I excuse myself, claiming I have to go pee, and sneak my phone into the bathroom with me. I've never even called him before. How strange is that? But I do have his number stored in my contacts, in case I ever needed to change or cancel an appointment. I bring it up, and chickening out, send a text instead.

-I know what I want. xo Belle

I sit in the bathroom for a full five minutes waiting for a response, but nothing comes. My heart sinks to the pit of my stomach as I wonder if, after everything, maybe he doesn't want me after all.

CHAPTER TWENTY-FOUR

~Trick~

I'm at the club, on my fourth tumbler of Booker's, and it's finally starting to numb some of the fucking ache in my chest. They weren't kidding when they said love sucks. It has certainly kicked me in the god damn balls today. I'm positive Belle feels the same as me, but fear is keeping her from moving forward. Or maybe, maybe I just pushed too hard, too much, and way too soon.

I take another swig from the glass, my eyes scanning the room. I didn't come here because I'm interested in fucking someone else, or because I want to forget everything in a beating. I came here because it's the one place I know won't smell like her. After our argument, I went home with Kane, and the minute I stepped into my apartment, all I could smell was that damn Burberry perfume. It was on my couch, my sheets, even my damn shirt.

This place is safe, the last place I know I'll ever have to worry about running into her. I lift the tumbler and drain the rest of the glass, signaling the waitress as she strides by. She knows I want the same, so she just nods and lifts a finger to let me know she'll be right back. And she is. Within five minutes, I have another drink in front of me. As I raise it to my lips, Samantha walks into my line of sight and sinks into the seat across from me.

"Hey, Trick." She places the wine in her hand on the table between us, her dark red nails clicking against the glass. "You need something tonight?"

"Nope." I swish the amber liquid in the tumbler around then take another swig. "All set."

"I bet I can make you feel a whole lot better than what's in that glass," she coaxes, reaching forward, covering my hand with hers, sinking her nails into my skin.

I snarl as I tear my hand out from under hers. "I said no."

She stands, sneering down at me. "You don't have to be a dick about it." Then she stalks away.

"Fuck you," I mutter under my breath, swigging more of my drink. My phone pings, and I turn it over to look at it, my heart ceasing its natural beat for several seconds before it starts racing. I read the text again, making sure the bourbon isn't playing tricks on me.

-I know what I want. xo Belle

I shove the chair back I rise abruptly. I pull a hundred out of my pocket, toss it on the table, and leave the club. I hail a cab, which takes ten fucking minutes longer than I want because it's seven o'clock on a Saturday night, but finally climb in and give the driver the address.

Twenty minutes later, I knock on her door, hoping like hell I'm doing the right thing by coming over here. The door swings open to a petite blonde with pink streaks in her hair laughing, a glass of wine in her hand. When her eyes land on me, her smile widens. "Well, you sure aren't the Chinese delivery unless they've upgraded." She giggles and holds up a finger.

"Oh, Annabelle!" she yells loudly. "Delivery for you." Then she turns back to me and crooks her finger for me to come in. "Patrick, I presume?"

I nod, my gaze swinging to the living room where another woman is rising up off the floor. She gives me a little wave when she notices I'm gawking at her.

"I'm interrupting," I stammer, not even considering Belle might have company over before I decided to just storm over here.

"Nope!" the blonde chirps. "We were just leaving." She swings her head to the other girl. "Weren't we, Krystal?"

"Yep!" she responds, both of them clearly leaving for my benefit.

"Don't go." I put my hands up to try to stop them, my head swiveling up just as Belle comes around the corner from the hallway, her wallet in her hand. As soon as her eyes lock onto me, her mouth drops open.

"I'm sorry," I blurt out before she can say anything. "I didn't realize you had friends over."

The little blonde cuts in again. "And we were just leaving." She waltzes over to Belle, whispers something in her ear, then pecks her on the cheek. "Come on, Krystal," she calls out to her friend, who's now standing beside me, pulling a sweatshirt over her head.

She snags Krystal's hand when she walks by, pulling her out the door, and winks at me as she does, whispering loudly, "Go get her!"

I chuff, surprised at her spunk, then spin my head back to Belle, who's now moved so that she's only a few feet away from me. I step completely inside the apartment and let the door close behind me. "I got your text."

"You didn't respond," she murmurs.

I shrug and take another step closer. "This is my response."

"Well, that's one way I guess." A small smile pulls at her lips.

"You said you know what you want," I state.

She takes another step closer, now only a few inches from me. "Yes."

"Tell me," I urge.

"You."

Before the word even reaches my ears, I yank her to me and slam my mouth over hers. Her hands wrap around my neck, grasping onto the nape of my neck, her body arching into mine. I cradle her face in my hands, consuming her, swiping my tongue across her lips, licking the inside of her mouth when she opens. She moans then mumbles against my lips, "You taste like whiskey."

"Bourbon." I chuckle, nipping her lip, sucking on it gently before sweeping my tongue back inside her mouth and sealing mine over hers. I continue to devour her, imprisoning her in my grasp, wanting to keep every inch of her against me.

She tears away from my mouth and nuzzles her head into the crook of my neck. "I'm sorry." She breathes against my skin, her grip around my neck cinching tighter. "I want you. I want us. All of it. I'm just so scared by how fast it's happening."

"Time doesn't matter, Belle." I squeeze her back. "Only what we feel. We'll figure it out as we go." I twist my head and brush my lips back against hers, my eyes locking onto hers. "I love you."

She gazes back at me, her ice blue eyes seeming to see all the way down to my soul, her lips curling up into a smile. "I love you, too, Patrick."

I crush my lips back over hers, claiming her once and for all as mine. I slide my arms under her legs, scoop her up, and begin walking to her bedroom. A knock on the door stops me in my tracks. We tear our lips apart and both look at the door. She looks back at me and starts laughing. "It's the Chinese. We ordered before you arrived."

Chuckling, I set her down. "That's the worse timing ever."

I stroll over to open the door and take the food from the guy. "Fifty-eight bucks, man."

Looking over my shoulder at Belle, I laugh and hold up the food. "Guess you girls were hungry?"

She comes over and takes it from me, giggling. "Three girls drinking wine. We like snacks."

I hand the guy a hundred, tell him to keep the change, and

slam the door as his jaw falls slack. Then I'm lunging for Belle. I throw her over my shoulder and carry her to the bedroom to consummate our love.

~

I check my watch as I ride up in the elevator to the twenty-third floor, cursing myself for being late. Her last appointment ended at eight, and it's now twenty after. I spent the morning at the hospital visiting Charlie, who gave birth to an absolutely beautiful seven-pound, six-ounce baby girl with a head full of chestnut colored hair. Trey was literally beaming with pride, so proud of both of his girls.

My afternoon was spent arranging for a packing and moving company for Belle, who agreed to move in with me. It's was happening in two weeks. We've officially been dating a little over two months and haven't spent one night apart since she told me she loved me. We have only grown closer, happier, and more content over that time. Nyla and Kane, not so much. But we are making it work, and I know, with time, they'll learn to live with each other.

I met up with Ben Sapphire at five-thirty to box and then went to a support meeting above the gym. Belle was right. It's helping. A lot. Ben has been instrumental in helping me to realize better, healthier ways to deal with my losses, my pain, and especially my guilt. Some days are still hard, but there are more good days than bad now. I couldn't get a damn taxi to save my life after the meeting, so I ended up taking the subway, and subsequently, am now late. I texted her to let her know, but I still hate to keep her waiting.

The elevator pings to a stop, the doors sliding open, and I stroll out, striding down to her office. I knock on the door once and enter. Her face lights up with a smile when she looks up from her desk.

"Hey, beautiful." I walk over and drop a kiss on her lips, leaning over the desk. "Sorry I'm late."

"No worries." She stands and walks around the desk. "How was the meeting?"

"Good." I pull her against me and brush another kiss over her lips, then look around the office. "I haven't been here in a long time."

"I know." She smiles coyly at me, striding away from me. At the door, she turns the lock before spinning back around to me. "I thought we could have a private session."

My cock springs to life under my jeans. My brow quirks up. "What'd you have in mind?"

She saunters back over to me, unbuttoning her blouse one leisurely button at a time, and stops when she's a foot in front of me. She swipes her tongue across her lips then yanks her shirt apart, her eyes locking onto mine.

"Holy fuck." I take a step forward, my fingers trailing over her chest. She's wearing a silver chain around her neck that drapes down between her breasts then wraps around her waist. But it's the two connecting chains that have my attention. They fall from the center chain, each one clipped to her nipples, which are red and swollen, protruding through the clip.

My dick is instantly hard. "You wore it." I gave it to her a week ago, keeping my promise to keep giving her 'more' but this is the first time she's worn it. She was so curious about how my nipple ring felt; I thought this would help her to experience it. I look up at her, wrap the center of the chain around two of my fingers, and tug, a low moan falling from her lips. "You're so fucking sexy."

I slide an arm around her waist and yank her up against me, thrusting my cock against her center as I walk her backwards. "I always wanted to fuck you on this desk."

She slams her mouth against mine, fisting my shirt at my waist, shimmying it up over my chest, tearing her lips off mine to pull it over my head. Her mouth surges forward, this time clamping onto my nipple, sucking hard, my cock swelling as she does. I reach between us and pull down on the chain, resulting in her teeth clamping onto my nipple, hard, as she whimpers. I lift her and shove her back on her desk then reach for the button of my jeans, flicking it open, then push them down my thighs.

My cock juts out between us, and I grin when I see her eyes lock onto it, her tongue swiping her lips again. I shake my head and step forward. "Uh-uh." I grip the bottom of her skirt and shove it up her legs, her ass lifting off the desk when I haul it up to her hips. "The only place my cock is getting buried is in your pussy."

She gasps as I grip her thong and rip it off her, stepping between her legs. I bend and suck one of her sensitive buds into my mouth, a yelp coming from her, her nails scratching into my back. I know how much it hurts, but I also know it's what she craves. I take my fingers and skim over her pussy, groaning when I feel how soaked she is.

When I let go of her nipple with a pop, she lets out

another cry, her body shaking beneath me. I grip my cock in my hand, slam my mouth over her open one, then shove myself inside of her in one stroke. Her back bows up off the desk, her core thrusting against me, her muscles clenching around me, so wet and so hot.

I buck my hips forward, slipping one hand behind her back to hold her in place, and slide my cock in as deep as I can. She falls back on the desk, moaning, her fingers clenched along the edge as I begin to heave back and forth inside her. I reach down and slide my fingers under the center of the chain and tug it toward me, pulling both of her nipples, stretching them tight. She tosses her head back and forth across the desk, her mouth open in a silent scream, her pussy pulsing around my cock.

I release the chain to grip her hips, surging even deeper inside of her, her orgasm triggering mine. Her name leaves me in a roar as I come, my release exploding inside of her. I loosen the hold I have on her hips and slide my hands under her back to lift her against me, our breaths both coming out in short gasps.

"That was fucking incredible," I pant out, peppering kisses against her neck.

"I should have let you do that two months ago," she says, both of us breaking out in laughter.

I slide out of her, pulling up my pants, and shove my cock inside before buttoning them up. "Hold on. I'll get you a towel." I walk into her bathroom and grab a fresh towel out from under the sink and bring it out to her. She wipes herself then I help her off the desk.

She looks down at her chest, frowning. "I'm kind of afraid to take these off." She raises her eyes to mine. "Is it going to hurt?"

I grimace, not wanting to lie, and nod. "Yep." I shake my head. "I should have taken them off earlier, when I was inside you. It would have all blurred together then. Sorry."

"Okay, just do it then." She leans back against the desk, thrusting her chest out to me, trusting me to take care of her.

I slide the closures for the clips down and release each of her nipples, one at a time. I palm a breast in each of my hands and caress them, bringing the blood circulation back to each nipple. She clenches her teeth, her body wriggling underneath me. "Yep, it hurts," she hisses out.

"I'm sorry." I bend down and put one of her nipples in my mouth, swiping my tongue back and forth gently, hoping to ease the pain a little.

She lets out a whimper. "That's actually turning me on."

I let go of her nipple and peer up at her. "Do you want me to stop?"

She nods but says, "No."

I chuckle. "Yes or no?" I swipe my tongue over the other nipple, waiting for her answer. "Cause, Doc, in a minute, they won't hurt anymore, and then time's up." I grin wickedly, remembering how I used that term on her in this very office to escape.

She sits up, pushing my head back with her hand, her mouth lifting into a smile. "Why you rotten little—"

I crush my mouth against her smile, our arms wrapping around each other, her body softening against mine. I pull away and bring my face to hers, my green irises finding her blue ones. "I love you."

She presses a kiss to my lips. "I love you, too."

"Come on." I lift her back off the desk and help her lower her skirt, then move my fingers up her blouse, fastening each button. "Let's go home."

CHAPTER TWENTY-FIVE

~Annabelle~

I'm not sure what I was thinking when I decided to have this housewarming party only two weeks after I've moved in with Patrick. I've barely had time to find a place for all my things, and now I'm rushing around the apartment trying to set everything up before our friends arrive.

"Patrick!" I shout from the kitchen.

His head pops out of the bathroom. He's being a champ and actually cleaning it. "Yes, dear," he drawls. I mean, to be fair, I may be freaking out a little and may have called his name over fifty times this morning.

"Where in the hell is the cutting board? Didn't you say you had a big wooden one?" I slam a cabinet door closed, not finding it.

He strolls out of the bathroom—adorable, I might add, with the yellow rubber gloves he's wearing—and points to a thin cabinet next to the stove. "All boards are in there." He cocks his head and gives me a small grin. "Same place they were last week when you used one."

I give him an impish smile and raise my arms in a shrug. "Sorry. Kinda freaking out here."

"Belle, it's going to be fine. These are our friends," he reminds me, not for the first time today.

"I know, but, Patrick, your grandmother is coming!" I reach down and yank the cutting board out of the cabinet. "Everything has to be perfect."

He chuckles, walking over to me. "Babe, you're here. It's perfect." He drops a kiss on my forehead then spins around and heads back into the bathroom. "Gotta go clean now, can't talk."

I giggle and then let out a long sigh. I need to chill out. I grab several different cheeses out of the fridge for the board I want to prepare and set them on the counter. There's a loud knock on the door, and my eyes fly up to the clock. It's way too early for anyone to be here yet. I stride over to the door, pull it open, then scream in delight. Krystal and Holly are standing there, and they both are loaded down with goods.

"Did someone say there was a party?" Holly beams brightly, walking past me, holding a large flower arrangement in one arm and at least two dozen balloons in the other.

Krystal follows carrying a box, kissing me on the cheek as she breezes by. "The cavalry has arrived!"

"I love you guys," I gush, a wave of complete gratitude washing over me. How lucky am I to have friends like this who know just what I need?

Krystal puts the box down and starts pulling items out—

beautiful cloth napkins, an embroidered table cloth, glass candle tapers, and an assortment of other similar items.

"You guys!" I stammer, my emotions getting the better of me. "Thank you so much. What would I do without you?"

"Well, this party would clearly suck," Holly jests. We break into a fit of giggles, me in relief more than anything else. Their very presence provides me with a whole new level of comfort.

Patrick appears from the bathroom, a smile breaking across his face when he sees the girls. "Thank God, you're here!" He sidles up to me, wrapping an arm around my shoulder, chuckling. "She's driving me crazy!"

The next hour is spent prepping, decorating, and finally, changing into more appropriate outfits for the party. Trey and Charlie show up first, which makes sense, seeing how they live one floor beneath us. I give them both a quick kiss then scoop the baby out of their arms, amazed by how much she's grown in just a month's time.

"Oh my gosh, how is it possible that she just keeps getting more beautiful?" I ask, peppering her little cheek in soft kisses. She smiles up at me, and I swear, I melt a little inside. Patrick slides up next to me and steals her out of my arms. "Let me see my future goddaughter."

He cradles her in his arms, rocking her, his eyes crinkling as he smiles down at her. "How's my little princess?" he coos over her.

"Hi, I'm Holly." She steps in front of me and extends her hand to Charlie. "Since this one seems to have forgotten her hostess manners." She looks over at me and giggles.

Charlie ignores her hand and pulls her into a hug instead.

"I'm so glad to finally meet you! Belle keeps talking about you, and I keep telling her we need to get together, and now here we are!"

"I've been a little busy, girls." I feign a glare in their direction. "Moving and stuff. Cut a girl some slack."

"Hey, I had a baby, so no excuses," Charlie quips, a smile on her face. She turns her attention back to Holly. "And this is my little princess, Karina Patricia."

I look over to Patrick, who's gazing adoringly at the baby. Yep, her middle name is after him, which turns him to mush every time he hears it. Karina is in honor of Karen, Trey's friend and pseudo grandmother.

"Did someone mention a baby?" Krystal appears, peeking over my shoulder. More introductions are made, and we all move into the kitchen area where I have appetizers set up. There's another knock at the door, and since Patrick has the baby, I go answer it.

I swing the door wide, smiling warmly at Gabby and Cameron, and not just because he's holding a case of champagne. "Oh my God, you brought booze. I love you!" I reach out and give her a hug. "Come on in."

Charlie made sure that Gabby and I made peace with each other a few months ago, sitting us both down before she had the baby. Gabby apologized for her behavior the night she showed up at the apartment, slightly drunk and even slightly more aggressive. Yes, it was a little awkward knowing she and Patrick had slept together, but I obviously knew he wasn't practicing choir boy behavior prior to meeting him. I was very sure that there was nothing but friendship between them anymore, especially after seeing her with Cameron Justice, her self-proclaimed savior.

Karen and Mrs. Connors, Patrick's grandmother, arrive together, completing the expected guests for our gathering. They are friends from way back who travelled in the same social circles, and can't be more delighted that they now have a reason to consider each other family. Karen gives me a quick peck on the cheek then heads straight to the baby.

"Mrs. Connors, it's so nice to see you again," I stammer nervously, accepting the bouquet of flowers she's holding out to me.

"Please, it's Colleen." She kisses me on the cheek. "I've told you before, no need for formality." She pats me on the shoulder. "Thank you for making my boy so happy." She turns and points to Patrick then looks back at me. "I've been worried about him for a long time."

"He makes me just as happy." I grip her fingers and squeeze gently. "You did amazing with him. He's one of the good guys."

"Yes, he is." We join the rest of the guests then and begin mingling.

The girls help me put out the lasagna, salad, and bread for dinner. Drinks are poured, then Patrick stands, tapping on his glass, clearing his throat. I had no idea he planned on making a little speech. I sit up straighter in my chair, anxious to hear what he's going to say.

"For a long time, I didn't think I'd ever find peace, let alone happiness." He swings his gaze to me and smiles. "Now, as I look around this table, I feel so lucky to have each of you in my life. You make it all the richer with your friendship and with your love." His cheeks flame, and he focuses on the table for a minute before looking up to continue. "So, yeah, thank you. Thank you for being here, for putting up with all my shit, and for helping me celebrate the next step in my life with Belle."

"Cheers!" I stand and raise my glass, my gaze locked on Patrick's, his shining green eyes staring back at me. And I know, without a shadow of a doubt, that the best is yet to come.

The End... for now.

Stay tuned for the next installment of
The Tempting Nights Romance Series,
Tempting Justice,
Gabby's story.
Releasing in April 2019.

AFTERWORD

The department of Veteran Affairs has disclosed that approximately TWENTY veterans a day commit suicide. Of these twenty, eighty percent are veterans, while the other twenty percent are active-duty service members, guardsmen and reservists. That equates to 6100 veterans and 1380 active duty service members a year. This number is not only staggering, it's heartbreaking.

Please, if you, or anyone you know, suffers from PTSD or has had thoughts about suicide, there is help. Someone is always available to listen. Please call one of the numbers below.

• National Suicide Prevention Lifeline (also affiliated with Mental Health America): (800) 273-TALK (8255). Available any time of day or night, 365 days a year, this toll-free PTSD helpline has trained volunteers standing by to provide crisis intervention, to offer support for people in distress, and to give information and referrals to people with PTSD and their loved ones.

• Veterans Crisis Line: (800) 273-TALK (8255) and press "1". This toll-free hotline is available for veterans and their loved ones. You can also send a text message to 838255 to receive confidential, free support and referrals.

• Crisis Text Line: Text HOME to 741741. This service is available 24/7 and provides free crisis support and information via text.

• National Hopeline Network: (800) 442-HOPE (4673). Available 365 days a year, volunteers who staff this toll-free hotline are specially trained in crisis intervention to provide support, information, and referrals to people in need. You can also access services via chat by pressing the "Chat Now" button on its website.

• PTSD Foundation of America, Veteran Line: (877) 717-PTSD (7873). Providing referrals, information, and helpful resources to veterans and their families, this toll-free hotline is available 24/7.

• Lifeline for Vets: (888) 777-4443. Also geared toward veterans and their families, this toll-free PTSD helpline provides crisis intervention, referrals, and information.

ACKNOWLEDGMENTS

Thank you as always to my husband and children. Without them, I would know nothing of love, and feel beyond blessed that they support and believe in me.

A big thank you to my book bestie and partner in crime, Haylee Thorne. She had to listen to me complain a lot during the writing of this story. I covered some deep topics and was so afraid I wasn't going to do them, or the characters justice. I couldn't ask for a better cheerleader, motivator, or friend. Love your face. Thanks for always keeping it real and for keeping me laughing when I want to cry.

To my book team: Amanda Walker, thank you for bringing Trick to life for me on this gorgeous cover, for all my teaser graphics, and for always having my back. You truly are my super squirrel, and I'd be a complete mess without you. Kendra Gaither, thank you for making my words shine. You accommodated my every schedule quirk, my endless concerns about warnings and content, and always had an ear when I needed to talk. You're so much more than an editor, and I'm so grateful to have you!

To the bloggers, the readers, my amazing author friends (you know who you are), and the best box of jewels an author could hope for, THANK YOU so much for your endless support, shares, feedback, and constant love you provide.

Last but not least, a huge thank you to my #drunkdivatribe. Meeting all of you has renewed some of my faith in this crazy book world. It can be a pretty dog-eat-dog place some days, and being able to share our struggles, our journey, our ups and our downs, all with laughter and love has been a god send. I can't wait for us to all soar through the stars and land on the moon together. Danielle, Sienna, Eva, Mia, Sonnie, Haylee, and Jill, thanks for bringing this chick into your tribe. Love you all hard.

ABOUT THE AUTHOR

Michelle Windsor is a wife, mom, and full-time writer who resides North of Boston. When she's not writing, she can usually be found with her friends and family playing a game of scrabble, watching the latest episode of Outlander, or cheering on one of her beloved Boston teams.

Stay up to date with Michelle on her website: https://www.authormichellewindsor.com

or on any of the sites below:

ALSO BY MICHELLE WINDSOR

The Winning Bid, Auction Series Book One

The Final Bid, Auction Series Book Two

Losing Hope

Love Notes

Tempting Secrets, Tempting Nights Romance Book One

Books Co-Authored with Haylee Thorne

Breaking Benjamin

Marrying Benjamin

Printed in Great Britain
by Amazon

28422053R00126